A KISS BEFORE THE WEDDING

They finally stood in the shade of the oak tree. "Isn't it magnificent?"

"I suppose," Bertram said.

"Let's sit down," Sorrow said, indicating the soft grass under the tree.

"But it is so damp! You will stain your pretty dress!"

"I don't care about that. Do . . . do you really like it? I wasn't sure . . ."

"It makes you look like a flower," he said, smiling finally. "It is almost pretty enough to do you justice."

She sighed happily. "You say such lovely things, Bert," she said, standing on tiptoe and kissing his cheek.

He took her in his arms and kissed her then, and she closed her eyes, surrendering to the sweetness of his mouth on hers . . . .

from *Sorrow's Wedding*, Donna Simpson

WITH THIS RING

SHANNON DONNELLY

JENNIFER MALIN

DONNA SIMPSON

ZEBRA BOOKS
Kensington Publishing Corp.
http://www.zebrabooks.com

ZEBRA BOOKS are published by

Kensington Publishing Corp.
850 Third Avenue
New York, NY 10022

All Kensington titles, imprints and distributed lines are avail-
able at special quantity discounts for bulk purchases for sales
promotion, premiums, fund-raising, educational or institu-
tional use.

Special book excerpts or customized printings can also be cre-
ated to fit specific needs. For details, write or phone the office
of the Kensington Special Sales Manager: Kensington Publishing Corp., 850 Third Avenue, New York, NY 10022. Attn.
Special Sales Department. Phone: 1-800-221-2647.

Zebra and the Z logo Reg. U.S. Pat. & TM Off.

First Printing: June 2004
10 9 8 7 6 5 4 3 2 1

Printed in the United States of America

CONTENTS

STOLEN AWAY

SHANNON DONNELLY

CHAPTER ONE

Was he never going to ask her the question?

Hands stilling on the arrangement of already perfect peach China roses, Audrey strained to hear Chloe's delighted cry. That would, of course, be Chloe's reaction to a declaration of marriage. Chloe never seemed to think of restraining any feeling, but perhaps this occasion merited such uninhibited enthusiasm. After all, why not be delighted about marriage to Lord Arncliffe?

Audrey let out a sigh. Then she frowned, and pulled her attention back to the moment.

Why no screech of delight, however muffled by the oak drawing room door? The hall clock ticked. A bird twittered in an empty-headed fashion in the back garden of the narrow London town house. And the faint rumble of carriage wheels echoed up from Half Moon Street.

Audrey edged closer to the drawing room. Were those Arncliffe's rumbling tones she could almost hear? Was he asking the question even now? Or was that Chloe talking too much again when she ought to be listening?

With another guilty glance around her, Audrey gave up the pretense on the roses and stepped closer to the door. *It is not really eavesdropping if I cannot hear anything, and if I do hear anything I shall move away at once as befits a lady.*

"Has he asked her yet?"

The hissed question startled Audrey into spinning about, the embroidered hem of her dress twirling around her ankles. She glanced up to the curving staircase that led to the bedrooms on the next floor. Her mother leaned over the cherry-wood railing, blue eyes bright and questioning. Her white lace cap sat crooked as usual over her dark brown curls, and she looked as if she had thrown on a purple-toned Paisley shawl at random over her green-striped muslin gown.

Her face hot, Audrey stepped away from the drawing room and met her mother as the older woman finished limping down the stairs, one hand on the banister and the other clutching a cane with an ivory handle carved into the shape of a horse's head.

Voice hushed, she said, "Really, Mama. We must not interrupt. And I wish you would allow Meg to aid you down the stairs in the mornings."

Mrs. Colbert wrinkled her nose and waved her free hand before taking her daughter's arm. "Meg fusses too much—more than you, even." She glanced at the door to the drawing room. "Are you certain he intends to ask her today? Most gentlemen seem to have a habit of sucking back under the bit when it comes to getting over the gate of matrimony."

Audrey had to smile. Hunting terms. Her mother's lapse into old habits, learned from a husband who had never spoken of anything but horses, meant she must be as nervous about Lord Arncliffe as any of them.

And why not? A marquess in the family, after all. The Colberts—country squires, all of them, including Chloe's father—had never aspired so high. But for a younger son, Chloe's father had wed well, marrying himself an heiress. And Chloe—beautiful, rich, orphaned Chloe—had captured Lord Arncliffe's instant attention.

Audrey had seen it happen.

Her throat tightened at the memory of that night—and of how Arncliffe had never even noticed her. But what gentleman had ever been able to look beyond Chloe's blinding beauty?

Audrey wrinkled her nose. She sounded as if she begrudged Chloe her success. And she did not.

No, she was happy for her cousin. Delighted. Utterly. How could there be a more perfect match? He would give Chloe sense and stability. She would give the rather serious marquess liveliness and no doubt children as golden as they were themselves. Everyone had remarked what a vision they made, with Arncliffe's rugged masculine features, Chloe's delicate feminine beauty, and both of them fair headed.

Yes, it *was* wonderful. And did not Chloe, who had already had too much sadness in her life, what with her parents dying three years ago on one of their endless trips abroad, not deserve such a blessing?

But uncomfortable feelings still stirred inside her, like bees loose under her skin. Of course Chloe deserved this. She needed this. Marriage would keep her from becoming a vain creature too aware of her beauty, too flattered by her suitors, and too caught up in fashionable frivolity. Yes, it would. Particularly since Arncliffe was so obviously smitten with her. Yes, she needed a loving husband. And did not all women dream of such a marriage to such a gentleman?

So why was her stomach in knots this morning?

For fear he would not ask? That must be it.

Forcing a smile, she took her mother's arm to lead

her to the small salon opposite the drawing room and spoke as much to reassure herself as anyone. "Lord Arncliffe would hardly have made the effort to see Great-uncle Ivor if he did not have intentions. I cannot recall the last time Uncle Ivor thought to send us a note about anything, and he did write us to expect Arncliffe's call this morning."

Mrs. Colbert nodded. "Yes. And I suppose Arncliffe does have a good stride on him, so we ought to rely on him to get over this smoothly. But . . . well, is this the right match for Chloe? She is only nineteen, after all. Arncliffe has a decade more experience of life."

"Exactly what Chloe needs—someone past his wild days."

For Chloe certainly is not.

She pressed her lips tight. She must not be so ill-natured. Any girl with such beauty as Chloe was bound to be a bit spoilt. Her parents, before they had expired, had provided their only child with schools, gowns, toys, and everything else. Everything but their time, it seemed. Audrey frowned. She would have loved to give Uncle James and Aunt Lavinia a piece of her mind about such an upbringing for a child—only they were far from this world's care now.

And Chloe had become her mother's concern, for Great-uncle Ivor, while he never questioned any of the cost to launch Chloe into Society, took little notice of anything outside his club and the whist table. That reminded her that she would have to get him to the wedding somehow to give the bride to Arncliffe. Perhaps the lure of whist at the reception? Yes. And she would have to make certain to invite some equally avid players.

She started to weave plans. A late June wedding. That would leave time for the banns to be called. And enough of Society would still be in London to make it

quite the event. Visions began to spin: vivid orange pe-
onies and white *Blanc Double de Coubert* roses with their
heavenly scent, ethereal bride clothes in pale yellow
silk. And Arncliffe, handsome in a black coat and satin
white breeches, sunlight glinting in his wheat-gold hair
and the faintest smile lifting his wide mouth as he
turned to his bride and . . .

Her mother's worried voice interrupted the fan-
tasy, "But what if Arncliffe thinks her too young?"

Audrey stared at her mother. "Why ever would he?
He thinks her perfect."

The words slipped out with a bite of jealousy that
even Audrey could hear, and she wished them back
at once. Her mother, however, only smiled and
squeezed Audrey's hand. "My love, you are worth a
dozen Chloes—and the gentlemen of London are
blind not to notice."

Audrey's lips twisted as her sense of the absurd
came to her rescue. "Darling, of course they have noticed me. How could they not when I stand
five-feet-ten in stocking feet, and have a figure that
would suit a maypole?"

Mrs. Colbert bristled. "You are tall and elegant!"

"Tall, certainly. With hair, indifferent brown, two
eyes, quite ordinary . . . "

"You have beautiful eyes! A true, deep brown. Your
father always said you had eyes as beautiful as his
mother's—and she was an accredited beauty!"

"But she did not have this nose, which looked far
better on Father than ever it became me."

Allowing her daughter to seat her on a sofa near the
unlit fireplace, Mrs. Colbert stared at her child. She
eased her gouty foot onto a footstool that Audrey had
pulled forward, then said, "There is nothing at fault
with the Colbert nose—it is a nose given down from
the Romans who settled Britain. And you've the bone

structure to carry it off—you shall be handsome into your forties and beyond, just as your father was. I will not have you belittle such gifts."

Audrey sat down next to her mother, back straight, hands folded in her lap, eyes twinkling. "Very well. Then I shall say that I have much to look forward to, and no fear for the loss of my youthful vanity."

Mrs. Colbert gave a small huff. "Vanity! I wish you had half of Chloe's—for the exchange would improve you both."

Instantly, she put her fingers over her mouth, her eyes widening. Then she pulled her fingers away again. "Oh, I ought not to say that about our Chloe. Not when the poor child has been through so much. I don't know what James was thinking to go to Switzerland, just to be swept up in an avalanche."

"He cannot have planned the snow to fall on him, Mama."

"James never planned anything in his life, least of all that. And now I am being horrid about my brother-in-law. It is just this waiting. I do hate waiting. Do you think you might step back into the hall and see if you cannot get some small idea of what is toward with Arncliffe and Chloe? They've been in there for over a quarter hour now—it never took your father that long to propose."

Audrey thought of her blunt, horse-mad father, with his rough manners and his jovial good nature. She could easily imagine him blurting out such a delicate question without the least qualm, not a care about a rebuff—or that he might be dragging a more sensitive soul into an awkward situation.

"*You won't ever be pretty, but by gads, I love you the same!*"

Jaw tightening, she pushed away the memory of his words to her—spoken so often, with such careless affection. Rising, she smoothed her skirts. At least he had loved her. Even if he had wanted a plump and pretty child—a child like Chloe.

Well, she had never been that. But she had also never been so willful and difficult. And perhaps the world was better for that. One Chloe seemed quite sufficient at times.

She smiled at her mother. "I'll just rearrange the roses again, shall I?"

"Oh, please do."

With her conscience eased, Audrey stepped into the hall. She had no need to move a single rose, however, for as she stepped from the salon, the door to the drawing room opened and Lord Arncliffe stepped out.

Audrey drew a breath and held it.

Did he look a man in love—a man made happy? Her mouth dried. Had she meddled in things she ought to have left alone? Or had she at least been able to bring him the joy he courted?

For a moment, he seemed not to notice her, but stood in the hall, turned slightly to shut the door behind him, giving her an attractive view of wide shoulders and his strong profile.

Sunlight slanted down from the upper windows, catching edges of silver in his wheat-gold hair. He was not a tall man—she could look him in the eye if he turned—but he carried himself with the aristocratic grace that spoke of early lessons in deportment and dance. His straight nose and deep set eyes gave him an aloof air, but she had often seen a warm humor light his eyes—deep green eyes, she knew, edged with flecks of brown.

As he turned, she noticed a dazed look in those eyes, as if he could not quite understand how he came to be where he was.

Her left hand clenched. Chloe could not have
been so foolish as to reject him, could she? Not a
marquess? Not Arncliffe? Not *him*?

Worry pushed her thoughts into words and she
blurted out, "She cannot have turned you away?"

CHAPTER TWO

Arncliffe stared at the elegant face and figure before him, his thoughts elsewhere and hardly recognizing the lady. Then her name clicked into place, and the polite habits drilled into him since birth took over. He gave a short bow.

"Not in the least—Miss Chloe has done me the great honor of accepting my offer." *And I sound a pompous oaf putting it that way,* he thought, hearing far too much of his stuffy father in the words.

Thrusting his hands behind his back, he clasped one in the other. Then he glanced at Miss Colbert again.

Audrey—yes, that was it. Chloe's cousin. They had met numerous times, but he had never noticed until this moment—with her standing in a slant of sunlight—that she had lovely skin. Pale, translucent skin without any flaw. Very pale, just now, he realized. And large dark eyes. Those he had noticed before. And had admired. He had never thought her a pretty woman, but she carried herself with an attractive ease, and those eyes seemed to hint at warmth and humor and . . .

And what was he doing admiring one woman when he had proposed marriage to another?

The collar of his shirt tightened to the point of

strangulation as his face warmed. He let go his hands to tug at his cravat, stopped the action, and glanced again at Miss Colbert. She stared back at him, looking as uncomfortable about this as he felt. Lord, she must be thinking her poor cousin had just committed herself to a dolt of a fellow. The other Miss Colbert—Chloe, that is—had certainly given him the impression he had gone about it all wrong.

"Do you not want to go down on one knee?" she had asked, just as he began to get the words out.

He had stopped his speech—the one he had so carefully rehearsed. The one in which he admitted his secret envy for the joy his brother had found with a love match that seemed far more valuable than any title or trappings.

He had stopped and stared at her. *"One knee?"*

She had smiled, soft dimples appearing beside the cherry-red bow of her mouth, and for an instant he had not been able to think of anything other than that mouth. Then she said, "Well, it is not very romantic with you just sitting next to me, now is it? Of course, a garden would be a better setting."

"Setting?" he repeated, his brow tightening.

"Far more romantic. With music in the background—that would be lovely. And a moon—moons are ever so romantic. And some divine intoxicating scent. I am not quite certain I like this rose water I bought—what do you think?"

She held up a slim, white wrist, waving it next to his face, the tapering fingers as delicate as fine porcelain. His mouth dried and he caught her hand. He just about went down on one knee for her, but it struck him how ridiculous a grown man would look in such a position. He also might knock one of the fragile side tables over with his boots, and how romantic would that be?

So he stayed on the sofa and pulled her closer. "Chloe, since the day I first saw you, I was struck by your beauty."

Smiling, she nodded. "Yes—most gentlemen are."

Distracted again, he frowned. Then he realized that it must be that dry wit of hers—the one so apparent in her letters, and the one she concealed so well under the guise of blandness required by Society in unmarried ladies.

"But it is not your beauty that caught my heart—it's your goodness, the sweetness that shines from within."

Chloe tilted her head, and her golden curls swayed to one side. "Really? You think me sweet? How charming." She leaned closer, and her voice dropped to a husky tone. "Is this where you crush me to your manly bosom because you cannot control your passion for me?"

He pulled back. "My manly what?"

She frowned. "You do have a passion for me, do you not?"

He let go her hand and dragged his fingers through his hair. None of this was going as he had thought it would. "Are you mocking me?" he demanded.

"Am I what?"

"I want to marry you."

Those cherry-red lips pulled into a pout. "Yes, I know. They all do. And it seems I am not going to get a garden from you. Or moonlight."

"I didn't know you wanted them until just now."

"Well, you ought to have, my lord. Honestly, you gentlemen! You have no romance in you!"

"So it's not romantic to lay my heart at your feet?"

Her smile softened. "Well, I suppose that is a little romantic."

His jaw set, he pulled out the ring he had bought for her—his mother had informed him years ago that she planned to be buried with the one his father had given her. He thrust the diamonds at her. "And choosing you a ring that's no match for your beauty is not romantic?"

Chloe's breath caught on a hitch. The trio of diamonds glinted, casting shimmering rainbows of colors into the room. "Oh . . . it's beautiful. And it's no match for me?"

Pleased he had at least done something right, he took her

hand. Her fingers quivered as he slipped the ring on the third finger of her left hand. Ah, so she did feel something. His shoulders eased. This had been her way of teasing him—of puncturing the pretension given him by the weight of his titles and his wealth.

Relaxing now, he smiled at her. "You are such a torment."

She glanced at him, eyes wide. Then a small furrow drew together dark golden eyebrows. "Am I?"

"Yes, you are, a fair torment. And I deserve it, for taking it for granted that you would accept me. I ought to have known better."

The frown deepened. "Really? Why?"

"Because of who you are. Because . . . what, have you forgotten already that first note you sent me?"

Chloe smiled. "Oh, but I so love it when you tell me what you think of my letters."

"You wrote that if we could see hearts instead of faces, we would judge this world differently."

"That's rather clever, isn't it?"

"You're clever. And I think that, when I read your note, that was the moment I started to fall in love with you." His smile faded. "What's in your heart, Chloe? Would you love me if I had no titles—no fortune? Nothing more to offer you than my honest love?"

She had been wiggling her fingers, watching the diamond glint, and now she glanced at him. "But you do have all those things. You cannot help having them. And I think I shall very much like being Lady Arncliffe." She giggled, then glanced at him. "Well, are you not going to kiss me? With violent passion?"

He had kissed her. He pulled her into his arms and kissed her, trying to be gentle, trying to express tender, sweet affection with the touch of his lips to hers.

Only somehow, when he pressed his lips to hers—why had it felt like kissing a statue?

Because she had stiffened? Because he had been a touch

intimidated by her perfection—that perfect mouth, perfect nose, those perfect eyes, and perfect curves that his hands had ached to hold? He certainly had held himself back, despite her quips about violent passion. She was, after all, a delicate young lady who had been sheltered from life. He had no wish to frighten her.

And when he pulled away, she had stared at him, eyes wide and that perfect mouth pulling down at the corners.

He had not been able to bear the look in her eyes—the disappointment.

But it was only an awkward first kiss, he told himself. He had done as poorly with his first mistress, had he not? And he had promised himself to move slowly. To take his time with this. Real love deserved such consideration.

Only why did he now feel so confused and put out about the whole thing? Just as he had at fourteen when he accidentally knocked over his mother's favorite Grecian statue, causing poor Athena to lose the only hand she had had left and getting him another of those agonizing sermons from his father on what he owed his name, his titles, and his position. As if any of that had to do with knocking over a statue.

Looking up at Miss Audrey Colbert, he realized now that he still stood in the hall, and that he had been staring into space. He had better manners than that.

He dredged up a smile. "It's a rather daunting thing to have just proposed and been accepted—and it has left me unaccountably dumbfounded. Do forgive me."

She came forward, her hand extended. "Oh, please. There is nothing to forgive. And, do . . . well, please allow me to be the first to wish you happy."

Smiling, he took her hand. Such a sensible woman. If not for her encouragement, he would not have hoped to win his Chloe. *His* Chloe. He could not stop his chest from puffing out. His titles and wealth had drawn other females, but such things ought to be of little importance to a woman of deep feelings and sensitivity. A woman such as Chloe. She had her own wealth, and beauty enough to lure a duke to her. But she had accepted him.

He glanced back at the drawing room, frowning, hearing again Chloe's voice as she rehearsed the title she would soon wear. That had been a bit odd for a woman who set so little value on such a thing.

A soft voice pulled him from his thoughts again. "No wonder you looked dazed."

He glanced at Miss Colbert. Then he smiled. "Would you—I told Chloe I would see myself out, but would you walk me to the door? I have a need for your counsel, if you will be so kind as to give it."

Swallowing hard, Audrey nodded, then started down the stairs, Lord Arncliffe at her side, a solid, unsettlingly male presence. She ought to have found an excuse as to why she could not help him—she really had no business acting as his confidant. Not with him now engaged to her cousin.

But she had not been able to resist that pleading look in his eyes.

"Miss Colbert—oh, confound it, if we are to be cousins, can it not be something simpler?"

Audrey smothered a smile. "Of course, my lord. As you wish, my lord."

He glanced at her, frowning. Then his expression relaxed. "You are teasing me, I hope. I do get fed up with all the pomp and privilege, however."

"Until you need to use it?"

He grinned. "Yes, until I need to use it. I am caught out as a hypocrite—if I wanted to be judged solely for myself, I ought to have styled myself Mr. Connor Derwent and had done with all the rest of it."

"But then you would have become the odd lord

who won't call himself for what he is. You would still have had a label around your neck, a far harder one for others to get around than merely being another marquess."

"Another marquess—I like the sound of that. As if we were as common as daisies on the road edge."

"You are, I assure you. Particularly this Season. It is just that you are marriageable, and marriageable marquesses are in short supply at the moment. Especially ones with a fortune and who are thought handsome."

His mouth twisted. "I would be thought handsome if I were eighty and had only one eye, so long as I also had my titles and the money to support them."

"True enough. But after you settle with Chloe . . ."

"I shall be envied then for my wife."

Audrey's smile froze. Then she said lightly, "Yes. Yes, you shall be. And a fine wife she will be for you."

Arncliffe stopped on the landing and turned to her. "Will she? And will I make a good enough husband for her? I am afraid I did all the wrong things—no bent knee, no moonlight, no music, and the wrong scent, even."

"Chloe said all that to you, my lord?"

"Please spare me from more titles and call me Connor."

"Very well—though I would rather not be Cousin Audrey. That has rather an old, grim sound to it."

He took her hand. "What if I call you Audrey—simply Audrey?"

She tried to make a joke of it. "Better than simple Audrey, I suppose."

"I fear I am the simple one. What is it that women think romantic, Audrey? Can you help me with that? What would Chloe think romantic? I failed her on the proposal, and I would rather get the rest of it right."

She parted her lips to tell him to forget such nonsense as moonlight and scents. What Chloe needed was guidance and a strong hand. But then she glanced at him and hesitated, doubt washing over her like a cold rain. She had been so certain of herself—so certain that she was doing good. Had she?

"Do you love her?" she asked.

For a moment, he stared at the dark blue runner on the stairs. Then he looked up at her. The mixed green and brown in his eyes made her think of deep forest glens, like those isolated enchanted ones from childhood tales. The faintest brush of gold flakes warmed the centers. "With all my heart, I love her."

Something twisted in her chest.

Looking down, she saw that he still held her fingers. Slowly, reluctantly, she pulled her hand away. She had to wet her lips before she could find her voice. "Then she is very lucky, and I can hardly advise you more than to continue as you are."

Turning, Audrey hurried down the stairs ahead of him. The porter jumped up from his chair beside the front door to hold out his lordship's tall hat, his tan gloves, and his mahogany walking stick. She turned to her cousin's husband-to-be, a smile pasted on her lips, her poise back in place. She could not let him see how those words had torn her open—she dared not. Oh, what a fool she was.

But at least she had the satisfaction of knowing she had done the right thing for him—and for Chloe.

"Why can you not write him for me?" Chloe protested. "You know how I hate when the ink stains my fingers—and it always spatters my gown! And I never think of the right words to put down until two days later—but you always think of them!"

Audrey turned from Chloe's wardrobe, where she had been selecting the gown for Chloe to wear tonight. "Because, cousin, I shan't be there forever to write your notes to him. And you must wish to express your thoughts and feelings. This is the most important occasion of your life!"

Frowning, Chloe held up her left hand. The diamonds on her finger winked in the candlelight. "Do you think that your toes ought to tingle when a gentleman kisses you?"

"No gentleman ought to kiss you unless he has proposed to you and been accepted—so you had best be speaking of Con—of Lord Arncliffe."

"Oh, I was—in a fashion. And do stop giving me that headmistress face, for it makes me feel I am back at that awful Miss Minton's Academy. Besides, I cannot help it if gentlemen always seem to want to kiss me."

"It is not the wanting that concerns me, it is the allowing. You are engaged now—to Arncliffe."

Chloe sat up on her bed and hugged her knees. "Yes—and it is quite lovely. I shall be Lady Arncliffe! And that wretched Miss Dunlow who thought she would catch him will be quite put in her place!"

Coming over to Chloe's bed, Audrey sat down, a white silk gown shot with gold clutched in her arms. "You do realize there is a man behind that title—a gentleman who cares a great deal for you. He is not a fish that you landed and should now parade to show your success."

"Oh, yes, I know. A fish is horrid and smelly." She gave a sigh. "But I do wish he could kiss better."

"Better? Save his learning to kiss you at all for your wedding night. Now come and get dressed, or you shall be late to dinner with his mother and his aunts."

Chloe watched, eyelids lowered, as her cousin rose from the bed. When Audrey turned her back, Chloe stuck out her tongue. Then she pulled it back and bit the tip of it. She ought not to blame Audrey for having to dine with a bunch of old ladies who would no doubt be boring and would fall asleep after the tea tray. Well, at least they could admire her ring.

Feeling better, she sat up, all smiles.

She had stopped smiling by the time she met Arncliffe's frosty mother and his staid, dour aunts. Stiff old biddies, far worse than she had expected. She had to put on her best manners, simpering like a ninny, keeping her eyes downcast, acting like a little dolt. The only spot of fun she had was when she winked at a rather dashing footman, making him blush. Of course, he could not keep his stare away from her for the rest of the night, and that put her in better humor.

Only Arncliffe did not even try to kiss her. Not once. No indiscreet whispers in her ears. No hot glances. No stolen presses of her hand in his wonderfully large ones.

He did look quite handsome, however, in his black evening clothes, his hair smooth as old gold. Though she wished that he did not always look so sober. And that he had dark hair. And not such hard features. However, when she glimpsed their reflection in the library mirror after dinner and saw how well they looked together, she almost forgave him for his restraint. She did so like men with broad shoulders.

But, lud, what a dull, dull evening.

Would every night be like this?

That thought swept terror into her as she sat in the carriage on the way home, wedged between her cousin and her aunt. They had come along, too, though Audrey had looked oddly pale and said hardly anything to anyone. Anyone might have thought she was sickening, only Audrey was never ill.

But Aunt Colbert was going on and on about such a beautiful house, and such polite company, and how Arncliffe was such a gentleman.

Chloe took a breath and forced her shoulders to relax. It could not possibly be like this every night. His mother would not live with them, nor would the aunts. Thank heavens his father had passed away years ago, otherwise he would not now be a marquess. And he did have a lovely house, with its own square even—Arncliffe Square.

Why had he not at least kissed her hand?

Wistfully, Chloe stared out the window, remembering a man who had not been a gentleman with her—a man who had taken the kiss he wanted from her. A searing kiss, his lips so warm and firm, his tongue coaxing open her mouth so that the jolt of intimacy at such a thing went straight through her.

He had also told her right after that he wanted her for her money, and that her good looks were just a bonus. When she had scorned him, he had laughed at her. His Irish brogue lifted his taunting words as he told her that he would have her anyway. She had been thrilled—and a little terrified. And had slapped his dark face, spun on her heel and run from him, away from the terrace where he had led her after their dance.

She had met him since, riding in the park, or at the theater. Sometimes he escorted other ladies. But always he came to her, staying away long enough to make her angry with him, then teasing her with his touches, with his assumption that she would have him.

Him? An Irishman? An obvious fortune hunter? Never!

But still he had watched her. And she had watched him as well. What if she had not run that night?

Only that rogue would not have made her a marchioness. He could give her nothing she really wanted. No position. No real security. She would always be fretting about his wandering eye, and would probably have to watch him fritter away her fortune.

No, she would marry Arncliffe. She would. And then she would stay away from his boring mother and his dull aunts, and she would make him make life fun for her. She would.

Even so, she fell asleep dreaming of black eyes and a dark-haired man with a glinting smile.

Audrey smothered a yawn as she opened the morning paper. She had always had breakfast with her father, she with *The London Times* and he with *The Morning Post*. She still had not given up the habit, even with him gone these past eight years.

However, the real truth behind her early rising of late was that she had been unable to sleep. And it showed on her face, she feared, in the dark circles gathering under her eyes, and the fatigue that even now numbed her mind.

But it would pass. Ten days had slipped away since the betrothal. The announcement had appeared in the papers. The vicar had only two more Sundays to call out and say that Connor Derwent, Lord Arncliffe, was to marry Miss Chloe Anne Colbert unless there should be anyone who could say why they should not marry. Of course, no one would ever say such a thing.

The invitations had gone out three days ago. And no one would think twice now of how tired she looked during the next fortnight, for everyone would be looking at Chloe, as they usually did. And she would be mercifully busy, for there were still flowers to choose, wines to order, decorations to arrange for the wedding breakfast afterward, and a dozen other things to keep one too occupied to feel anything other than exhaustion.

She heard her mother's cane thumping—fast and unsteady—and she put down her paper. What was wrong?

Panic tight in her chest, she started for the door as her mother came in, still in her nightcap and billowing dressing gown, her cane tight in one hand, and waving a note in the other hand. "She's gone— Chloe's gone. I think she's been abducted!"

CHAPTER THREE

Audrey almost laughed, it sounded so absurd. Only her mother's expression did not look the least teasing—not with her cheeks flushed and worry glazing her eyes.

Taking the crumpled sheet from her mother's trembling fingers, she scanned the black, strong hand scrawled across the vellum as her mother's words tumbled out. "It's that Irishman. It must be. He's the only Fitzjoy we know! Oh, I ought to have warned Chloe against him!"

"You did, Mother. So did I. As well as warning him off as best as possible," Audrey said, then rubbed the knot between her eyebrows. She could box Chloe's ears for having proven such easy prey—running off to meet him at a midnight masquerade. Of all the silly things! A sick knot tightened in her stomach. She looked up from Fitzjoy's note and glanced at the gilt-edged clock set on the carved mantel. Gone seven hours already. The girl would be ruined if word of this became known.

Glancing at her mother, she asked, "How did Fitzjoy get this to Chloe? Was it through Meg?"

"Oh, but you cannot blame poor Meg if she is a touch foolish."

"I can and I will dismiss her for her folly if this destroys Chloe's life! I specifically told Meg about Fitzjoy the first time I intercepted one of his missives. The man's a blackguard! For all we know, Chloe is already . . . already . . ."

"Please do not say it! We must hope that fence has not yet been jumped. But if it has, what are we to tell Arncliffe?"

Taking her mother's hand, Audrey led her to the round cherry-wood breakfast table, seated her, and poured her coffee. "Drink this, love, and do not distress yourself further. Fitzjoy must have marriage in mind, which may be her salvation, for it means a long carriage ride to Scotland. And you know how she is in a closed carriage."

A faint smile lifted Mrs. Colbert's mouth. "Oh, yes. Yes, I had not thought of that. That will slow them—but what are we to do? I supposed we ought to send for Uncle Ivor and—"

"Uncle Ivor? I cannot see him stirring his bulk from his club, not even for this disaster. And if we are to avoid scandal, there must be as little said about this as possible."

"Does that me we must accept Fitzjoy as Chloe's husband? How very uncomfortable a relation that shall be."

Audrey threw Fitzjoy's note onto the table. She saw her duty clear, and seeing it made her want to throttle her cousin. Of all the—

She caught the recriminations before they could fully form. Fuming wasted time. Starting for the door, she called back, "Tell everyone—even that simpleton Meg—that Chloe and I had to leave town of a sudden. Better still, I shall impress upon Meg the story I want her to know."

Mrs. Colbert plucked the note from the table. "But what of this?"

"Oh, just say that Chloe departed with me after returning from that foolish masquerade."

"Buy why would she—or you—gallop off like that?"

Pausing at the door, one hand on the cold, brass knob, Audrey waved her other hand, desperation tightening around her chest. "Darling, can you not make up some elderly, invalid relative, and some dreadful immediate illness?"

"There's her Aunt Sylvie."

"She'll do."

"But she's quite a healthy sixty."

"Then have her struck by lightning—or something else startling. I really cannot think of what just now."

"But wherever will you be?

Audrey offered a grim smile, then said, "Where else—chasing after Chloe!"

With her face turned toward the carriage window and her scented handkerchief pressed to her mouth, Chloe struggled for control over her body.

The voice, so melodious with its hint of Irish lilt, came from the opposite corner of the coach, a touch of amusement in the tone, and scraped across her nerves like a knife across slate. "Sulking still, dear one?"

Dragging the handkerchief from her lips, she shot the man a glare. "Do not speak to me, you . . . you . . ."

Stomach churning, she turned away again, pressing the lace to her mouth as she muttered, "I wish I were dead."

He laughed. *Laughed!* She glared at him again over the froth of lacy handkerchief. But he only lounged against the worn leather seat, his arms crossed, his long legs, still in black evening breeches, white stockings, and dancing pumps, stretched before him. "Now, now. You had your ball, did you not, as I gave you my word you would."

"Your word!" She made a rude sound and turned away. "You may at least have the decency to open a window!"

"What—so you can scream rape, is it? You'll have to wait for that. Least 'til we've stopped for the night."

Tight lipped, she glared at him. How had she ever thought that mocking face handsome? In truth, he had too swarthy a complexion. And too narrow a face. Lanky. Yes, he was lanky. Black hair spilled forward, falling into his eyes, unfashionably straight, and now she saw that he must have a heart as black as those inky eyes of his.

"Very well. Then I shall be ill inside the coach," she said, then pressed her handkerchief to her mouth. The scent turned her stomach so she wadded the lace in a fist and threw it to the opposite side of the coach.

His easy smile faded. Then a flash of white, even teeth brightened the coach. "Try again, now. I'm not some green one who'll believe such a story as that."

Swallowing hard, Chloe pressed her hand to her mouth even harder, but she would loose the battle soon enough. Sweat beaded cold on her forehead. She hated traveling. Hated what swaying in a closed coach did to her. Hated how her head pounded and her insides churned. *I warned him,* she thought. And then the wave of nausea swept through her and she wanted only relief.

He must have seen the truth in her face or her eyes, for with a muffled curse, he sat up, moving faster than she would have thought he could, leaning across her to struggle with the latches to the glass window.

The bile rose. With a hiccup, she choked it back once. Her throat burned. She hated being ill.

With another curse, he gave up on the window and threw open the door, yelling at the coachman to stop.

She no longer cared. His hands wrapped around her to lift her down, but she could do no more than turn and be sick onto the opposite seat. And then she burst into choking, hot-faced tears.

"Ah, sweet Jaysus. I would pick a bloody heiress who can't keep down her accounts."

Eyes watering, sniffling now, Chloe pushed past him, stumbled out of the coach and staggered onto the grass verge of the road. Dawn lit the eastern sky. She glanced at it, hating it, hating herself, but most of all hating this Irishman who had promised her a masquerade ball—and then had spirited her away and into the night.

Turning, she fisted her hands and propped them on her hips. "I want to go home."

One black eyebrow cocked. "Too late, dear one. It's a night we've been together in this coach, and you'll wed me if you care to be welcomed again by anyone in the polite world."

She wiped her fingers across her cheeks, brushing aside the tears. Her hair clung to her forehead, her curls limp. The stiff brocade of her masquerade gown—she had gone dressed as a shepherdess—itched. She wanted a bath, hot tea to settle her stomach, and her own bed.

"Take me home," she demanded again, stamping her foot this time on the soggy grass. "I want to go home!"

Rolling his eyes, he lifted his palms, then turned away, cursing. Glancing back at her, he scowled, and the expression on his dark face almost made her wish that she had not made him angry. "Well now, and just how do you think to manage that in a coach that stinks worse than the back mews of a tavern?"

She glanced into the coach. Then shuddered. She could not—would not—get back into it. Looking around her, at the green of the countryside, she took in the wild oxeye daisies and yellow cowslips in the field opposite the road, the tidy stone wall that divided pasture from lane, the birdsong and the distant bleating of sheep.

She glanced at the man who had brought her to this—who had taken her away from her home. Who wanted her ruined! What did it matter if she made those black eyes flash with anger and that unsettlingly attractive mouth pull down? She did not care if she displeased him.

Folding her arms, she lifted her chin. "You had best go and fetch something in which you can convey me home!"

He stalked to her side. The breeze lifted the lock of black hair from his forehead, stirring the soft strands. "Have you not heard a word I've said, or is it just that you're a bit slow?"

"Slow!"

"Your home's with me now—or it will be soon as you're my dear Mrs. Fitzjoy."

Her mouth dried and her pulse quickened as he loomed over her, solid and masculine and rather daunting, those black eyes now glittering like shards of black ice. But she would not be cowed. Not when she felt so miserable. However, she had to lift her chin a little more to keep it from trembling.

"I am not marrying you! I am going to be Lady Arncliffe! I only went with you last night to have a bit of fun before I married—not to run away with you!"

He grinned. Then he caught her around the waist, pulling her to him with an abruptness that took her breath. The glitter in his eyes quickened, as did her pulse. She braced the heels of her palms against unyielding muscles. Would he kiss her? Now? On the road? In the mist of a rosy summer dawn?

"I've a way of changing a maid's mind about such things," he said, the rumble of his voice vibrating through her. Then he let her go and pinched her chin. "But first, dear one, we need you smelling a bit better than you do."

He turned away to saunter up to the driver, leaving her alone on the edge of the road, the morning dew soaking her silk slippers, her stomach no longer heaving, but now as hollow as if she were a porcelain doll. And the disappointment sharp.

With a low growl, she stomped one foot. It made no sound on the grass, so she called out to him, "I hate you!"

And then she began to plan how to make his life an utter misery. Before he could make hers one.

Audrey thought about sending the footman to hire a traveling chaise, for they kept only a single pair of horses and an open landau with a canvas top that could be put up in bad weather. However, the footman would then know that she and Chloe had not left the house together. And if one servant knew, the entire house would soon hear the story—and servants from one house talked to servants from other houses.

She could not risk it.

Not if Chloe were to be extracted from this without talk, and without Arncliffe learning the truth. He might, of course, be gentleman enough that he would still hold to his betrothal to Chloe, even in such circumstances. But such knowledge must wound his pride and his heart. She would not allow that. No, somehow she must fetch Chloe back—hopefully repentant for her folly, but otherwise unharmed.

That meant, of course, hurriedly slipping a few things for herself—and Chloe—into a small portmanteau that she could carry and slipping out of the house at once.

A short, sharp questioning of Meg had at least made it clear that Chloe had left with no more than the clothes on her back. She must not have planned an elopement—so Fitzjoy had abducted her.

Well, he would be made to suffer. Abduction, particularly of an heiress, carried grave penalties. Only how could Great-uncle Ivor prosecute the fellow without the story becoming known? Well, she would save that threat for if the worst had happened to Chloe.

Her throat tightened. She smoothed a hand down the front of her short spencer jacket, her fingers brushing the mother-of-pearl buttons. The worst could not have happened—or so she prayed. She would cling to that thought, and she would bring Chloe home. Intact.

Taking a deep breath, she took up her soft-sided reticule, her York tan gloves, and a chip straw bonnet and slipped down the stairs and out the front door. A note given to the tearful and repentant Meg to hand to the porter had sent that servant elsewhere in the house on another task. Now she would have to hope that her mother carried off her part of the story well enough to convince both the staff and any callers.

At least Meg, guilt-ridden as she was, had been rehearsed into forgetting anything she knew about Chloe's adventures.

Once outside the house and on Half Moon Street, Audrey hesitated. She knew that various mail coaches left from various inns, but she had no idea which ones they might be, nor if these establishments hired out traveling chaises. They must, she assumed. But servants had always been sent to make such arrangements. She simply gave orders.

Biting her lower lip, Audrey glanced up and down the quiet street with its tidy, flanking rows of prosperous town houses. A breeze ruffled the hem of her skirt. The sun had not yet risen high, and deep shadows from the plaster-covered buildings cast a chilly shade over her. She shivered. Should she have worn something more sturdy than a blue muslin day dress, even if it did have long sleeves, and the short jacket, which buttoned at the high waistline of her gown? Well, walking would warm her. And if she saw a hackney, she would wave the driver down. Barring that, she could certainly make her way to one of the better hotels.

At that, she brightened.

Brown's! That would be just the thing. They knew her and her mother at that respectable establishment. The hotel porter could summon a vehicle for her, and she had the household account money in her reticule to pay for the service. She hoped that eighteen pounds, five shillings, and tuppence would be sufficient. If not—well, she would think of something then.

Putting down her portmanteau, she pulled on her gloves, settled her bonnet in place, and tied the ribbon under her chin. She would manage. She must. For Chloe's sake. For her mother's. For Arncliffe.

She frowned again. She rather hoped he and Chloe had not had any engagements set for the next day or so.

Bending down, she took up her bag.

As she straightened, a carriage turned the corner

from Piccadilly—a black phaeton with a high perch seat and four smart, matched grays.

She glanced at it, worried. Could she avoid notice? Turning, she tucked her chin down and started up the street, hoping the brim of her bonnet would obscure her features.

Behind her, the clop of hooves on the hard dirt of the street stopped. She glanced back.

The four thoroughbreds stood before the town house that her mother had rented for the Season. A short, stocky groom stood beside the leaders, settling the animals, smoothing a hand over first one gray dappled neck, then another. White manes fluttered in the breeze. Then the gentleman driver leaped down from the high-perch seat. The broad shoulders and the glimpse of gold hair from under his hat betrayed his identity—Arncliffe!

Of course. Who else would call so early in the day, as if he were family?

Biting back a groan, Audrey started to hurry away, but he had already glimpsed her, for he called out, his tone uncertain, "Miss Colbert?"

She slowed her steps. It would be unforgivably rude to pretend that she had not heard, but she had a craven desire to do just that. Instead, she turned.

A smile lifted his lips as he started toward her. He took off his hat as he reached her side, sweeping a polite half bow.

Audrey swallowed. She swallowed again.

What in heavens would she tell him? And how could she explain why she was walking down the street with a portmanteau in one hand?

CHAPTER FOUR

Taking in the startled look in Miss Colbert's eyes and the bag grasped in her hand, Arncliffe asked, his tone intentionally flippant, "Running away from home?"

Instead of smiling at his jest, her eyes widened and her shoulders jerked, as if he had cracked a whip in front of her face. Did she disapprove of his levity?

She must not, for she curved her lips into what seemed meant to be a smile, but those expressive brown eyes of hers betrayed a haunted edge of nervous worry over something. She wet her lips, then said, "Oh, the bag—yes. I'm . . . just off to pay a call. On a friend."

He stared at her, trying to keep his features blandly polite. The excuse sounded as odd as her forced tone. A visit? At this hour? But he always rose unfashionably early himself, so how could he fault her for the same sin? Still, he could not shake the sense that something was amiss.

Keeping his tone light, he said, "Well, I cannot allow a lady to continue on foot—not when I've a carriage at hand. Please, allow me to escort you."

He leaned forward to take her bag. He wrapped his hand over hers, expecting her to relinquish her hold. She did not, and so they stood there, her hold-

ing the bag, and him holding her hand. *We must look
ridiculous,* he thought. Only it did not feel so, not
when he stood close enough to catch the sweet-tart
scent of orange blossoms—what must be her scent—
and close enough to see the faintest of freckles
dusting her cheekbones. They gave her the charm of
a schoolgirl.

The color rose into her cheeks as she stared at
him. "I could not impose, my lord."

"I thought we had progressed to Connor and Audrey? And why can you not impose—*cousin?* We are
as good as related already, and what other use do relatives have, other than to be imposed upon, so they
might return the favor?"

She wet her lips. She had a generous mouth, he
would say, though at the moment it pulled down into
a frown. But the lower lip curved ripe and lush and
was made for more than smiles.

"I . . . well, my friend is ill and I am just taking her
a few things. But thank you. It is kind of you to offer."

Puzzled, he released his hold. Why was a footman
not carrying her bag for her? Why did she not have
her carriage waiting? A half dozen more questions
formed, but too many years of training as to manners
held them in check. So he only said, "Very well. I
shall just call on Chloe, for I promised her a morning dri—"

"Chloe? But you cannot!"

Startled by the urgency in her voice, he stopped
his movement toward the town house, and then
asked, his forehead bunching tight, "Is she still abed
then? She swore to me she always rose early, no matter how late the hours she kept the night before. We
made a wager on it, in fact."

"Yes, but—she . . . she is not at home just now."
The breeze lifted and tugged her bonnet back to re-

veal a spill of brown curls. With her free hand, she crushed the chip straw into place, but one lone curl dangled over her left eyebrow. She looked even more the guilty schoolgirl now, caught in some misadventure.

"Not at home?" he asked, startled into the question. "But where is she then?"

"She . . . went to visit a friend of ours, and she is now there, too, and sick . . . as well."

"Something that contagious sounds rather dangerous."

She shook her head, and the bonnet started to slip again. It was, he thought, an annoyance of a bonnet, with its deep brim and only a plain blue ribbon around the yellow chip straw. She crushed it into place once more. "It is not serious. She is far improved. But, she . . . Chloe would be embarrassed if anyone were to see her just now."

Concerned and bewildered, he asked, "Do you mean to say she has the measles or something like?"

"Yes—that is exactly it. Measles. She went just the other day to visit her friend, and now she must stay until she is better. Which ought to be only a matter of a few days."

His mouth quirked. He could, of course, tell her that he did not believe one word she had just uttered. But that would be boorish of him. And she had his curiosity now well caught. Why could he not see Chloe? Where was Audrey going with that bag of hers? And what might she say next if he pressed her?

He kept his expression schooled, and he hoped his eyes did not betray his lack of faith in her tale. "I did not think measles started up so quickly, nor ended so fast. But are you not afraid of catching them as well?"

She stared up at him, and he could see her mind

working—those wide brown eyes betrayed the glitter of thoughts turning rapidly. Then she said, "I had them as a child."

With that, Audrey bit the inside of her lower lip. At least it was the truth.

Arncliffe still did not look inclined to accept this excuse and go away—that stubborn chin of his! Instead, he said, his tone sounding grave, "It still is a disease that can turn dangerous, what with fever and all. I really must insist on sending my doctor to—"

"Please, no! I mean, it is very kind of you to think of Chloe, but she and her friend . . . our friend . . ." Oh, she sounded half addled. Taking a breath, she pushed her fraying nerves into order. "Our friend, Mrs. Fitzjoy, lives too far north to make it an easy journey, and I am certain they have a physician in attendance already. So I really cannot bother you further about this."

Putting on her best, most charming smile, she prayed, *Oh, please, go away now.*

Only his mouth had pulled into a resolute line, and she did not know what to make of that odd, knowing look in the depths of his eyes. But what could he say? She knew him to be far too much the gentleman to accuse her of lying—and she had indeed stretched the truth beyond recognition. Her throat hot, she swallowed. Her cause must justify her actions.

And she honestly would box Chloe's ears when she caught up to her. Right after she finished with Fitzjoy!

Leaning forward, Arncliffe took her bag from her, this time with such command that it had gone from her grip before she could even tighten her fingers about the handles. "That settles it. I cannot allow my betrothed's cousin to be jaunting about England without escort to someplace so distant."

Turning, he settled his tall beaver hat on his golden hair, then offered her the crook of his arm. She struggled for another excuse and found only the weight of her lies pressing on her. Well, she had certainly earned a just reward for digging herself this hole. She could see no option other than to allow him to escort her somewhere.

She glanced at his team. At least they looked to be fast, and she could use speedy transportation to an inn where she might hire her own carriage. When the time came, she would just have to think of some excuse as to why they must part company.

And then she would have to hope that she caught up with Fitzjoy and Chloe well south of the Scottish border.

He had hired a farmer's gig, a tawdry, narrow-seated carriage, its varnish faded away in spots, with a single dull-coated bay gelding put between the shafts.

Sniffing back her last storm of tears, Chloe stared at the ugly vehicle and the long-eared, placid gelding attached to it. "I am not riding in that!"

"So it's walking you'd rather?" he asked, his smile back in place. He had come back whistling, driving the gig. He had paid off the other coachmen, sent them away, and then had tried to usher her into that awful gig as if it were a royal carriage.

She folded her arms. "I cannot be seen in that in London."

His eyes danced with devilment. "Oh, you'll not be, dear one. I'll swear to that."

"If that means you do not intend to take me to London, then I—oh, what are you doing? Put me down at once! I said—ohhhh! Why, you . . . you . . . you ruffian!"

Chloe struggled to right her clothes after being lifted from her feet and tossed onto the gig's hard seat as if she were baggage. Before she could do more than straighten her evening cloak and skirts, Fitzjoy vaulted into the carriage and sat down next to her. If he had not already dismissed the other carriage and its drivers, she would have screamed to them for help.

Turning, she started to climb out the other side of the gig, but something yanked her back. She twisted and found that he had tucked part of her cloak and masquerade dress under him, so that he sat on the velvet evening cloak and part of her white and gold brocade shepherdess gown.

With a sharp tug, she pulled at the fabric. It stayed where it was under his black evening breeches.

He leaned towards her and smiled. "Sit still and enjoy yourself. It's not far you'd be going, walking in those pretty slippers of yours, after all."

Folding her arms, she turned away to give him her profile. "I hate you!"

She heard him cluck to the gelding and the gig lurched forward. "Do you now? We'll see if you're saying the same tonight still."

She glanced at him, then put her head back, pulled in a breath, shut her eyes, and let out the longest, loudest scream she had.

The gelding startled forward at the screech, and Fitzjoy cursed. Then his arm tightened around her waist and he dragged her to him, crushing his mouth over hers, his lips hot and his tongue dazzlingly clever. She half lay against him, her scream stopped, her breath ragged, her head spinning.

Then he pulled back, and her eyes opened. She

stared into those black eyes of his with their dark, liquid, endless depths. His breath, as rough as her own, brushed her face.

With a grumbled curse, he pushed her back onto her seat. "Behave now, or I'll give you something worth screaming over."

Frowning, she stared at him, her heart beating far faster than the gelding's brisk trot, and trying to re-orient herself. The world seemed to have turned itself inside-out during that kiss. Had he not felt the same?

Her lips still burning, she lifted one eyebrow. "You wouldn't dare!"

His eyes glittering and his voice a low growl, he told her, "I've dared everything for you . . ."

Her lips parted. A quick warmth spread through her. Would he kiss her again?

Then he spoilt everything by adding, "For you and your fortune!"

With a frustrated snarl, she hit him.

He only grinned, then caught her wrist as she started to draw back her hand to hit him again. "Ah, now, that's enough of that if it's a soft bed and a hot meal you want tonight. Otherwise, it's an empty barn for the both of us and you'll spend the night wrapped up as tight as could be."

Jerking away from him, she folded her arms and turned to stare at the countryside. Tears stung the back of her eyes, but she would not allow them to fall. She hated him. Hated.

But why then could she still feel that kiss tingling on her skin? And why did she want to provoke him into kissing her again?

She chattered. Arncliffe glanced at the woman next to him, his lips pressed tight, torn between a longing to beg her for silence, a simmering amusement, and the utter pleasure of letting that voice wash across him. Thankfully, she had a low-pitched voice, as rich as wild honey.

But two hours of any voice could wear, particularly when rattling on about the proliferation of daisies and cowslips in the pastures, and the dazzling white woodruff growing under the oaks. She had also offered inane speculation on how long the blazingly fair skies might hold, and noted the charm of Finchley Common—which seemed more common than charming to him. And she asked odd questions about carriages they passed, speculating on their destinations, their speed, and how frequently one might wish to change horses to make the best time on the road.

He could almost suspect she wanted to give him a dislike of her company. But why? So that he might set her down?

At the Tyburn Turnpike and then at the Islington tollgate she had also put some rather odd questions to the gatekeepers, even asking one fellow, "Why, you must meet all sorts passing through—even perhaps an Irishman?"

The fellow had scratched his head, offered as he supposed he might, but no Irishman of late that he could recall, and then, after Arncliffe's groom tossed him the shilling and sixpence to pass, he lifted the gate and waved them through.

Just beyond Barnet, and near to twenty miles now, the village of Hatfield, with its posting inns and cottages, came into view. Arncliffe almost sagged with relief.

Instead, he interrupted Audrey's ramblings. "Do you care to take refreshments while I have the team changed here in Hatfield?"

She glanced at him, clutching her bonnet with one

hand. The breeze from the road had flushed her cheeks an attractive pink. "Hatfield? Oh, but this is where I am to meet Mrs. Fitzjoy. I had not thought to arrive so soon. Do please stop—yes, there at . . . at The Swan, please. Yes, that is where I am to meet Mrs. Fitzjoy."

He glanced at her, fighting a smile. Then, obedient to her request, he gave his attention to getting his team into the stable yard. "I thought your Mrs. Fitzjoy lived a good deal north and that she was ill."

Her voice seemed the faintest touch clipped with irritation as she answered, "This does seem a good deal north when one is living in London. And she will have a carriage waiting for me."

Halting his tired team—the horses sweaty and ready for a rest—Arncliffe let the reins drop. Joe, his groom, had already swung down from his perch behind the seats to go to the heads of the leaders, and the stable lads from the inn came forward to help unbuckle the harness.

Arncliffe turned to his passenger, wondering what story she would offer him next.

Instead, she gripped his arm, her eyes suddenly dark and intent. "Thank you. Thank you so much. But we must part ways here. Really, we must."

With that, she turned and scrambled down from her seat, taking her portmanteau with her. And then she strode into the inn, her head up and her back straight.

He stared after her, torn between the desire to help her and the dictates drilled into him from his early years. *A gentleman never intrudes, never puts himself into the business of others. A gentleman respects a lady's honor above all else and never questions her.* He could almost hear the platitudes in his father's droning voice.

And he was damned tired of following them. Particularly when this stubborn, independent lady looked to be deeply troubled by some problem.

He swung down from his seat, then gave orders to his groom to see his grays rubbed down and watered—he would arrange later for them to be fetched back to town—and to oversee the selection of a new team.

That done, he made for the inn. Was there really someone here to meet her? And if that tale unraveled, what one would she spin for him next? It surprised him just how much he looked forward to discovering the next steps in this dance.

After the bright sunlight of summer, the low-ceilinged inn with its wood paneling seemed dark. He paused on the threshold to allow time for his eyes to adjust, anticipation tingling on his skin.

The scent of tobacco and ale drifted to him from the tap room, along with the welcoming aroma of meat roasting in the kitchen. The faint, low hum of the grooms' conversations carried to him from the yard, along with the jingle of harness and the clop of hooves on cobblestones.

Then he heard her, that distinctive contralto, its tones rich and no longer rambling but sharp with command. "What do you mean you have no carriage that the likes of me might hire?"

Arncliffe smiled. Well, perhaps now he might get a truer story. Then he stifled his smile and stepped forward, making certain to make enough noise to announce his presence.

CHAPTER FIVE

Even before she heard his boots on the wooden floorboards, Audrey sensed his presence in a prickling of awareness that swept down the back of her neck. She turned, her irritation with the innkeeper settling onto Arncliffe as well. Why must a single female be regarded as helpless or dangerous? These two did nothing but delay her!

She caught herself on that. In truth, Arncliffe had not delayed her—but having to invent more explanations for him certainly would. And she feared Fitzjoy and Chloe were already too far ahead.

Then Arncliffe swept off his hat and swept the situation from her control. "A private parlor, if you please," he said to the innkeeper. "And something cool to drink—lemonade for the lady. I'll have ale."

The innkeeper bowed, then bowed again as he hurried to open a door into a small parlor with sparse furniture and white curtains at the windows. After seeing them into the room, he bowed again and hurried off, attentive to Arncliffe's orders as he had not been to hers.

Insufferable, really, that a single female who wished to hire a carriage should be treated as a pariah, while a prosperous gentleman with an air about him could command the world. With her tem-

per simmering at such injustice, Audrey strode about
the room, then sat down in one of the four wooden,
straight-backed chairs.

"I thought we parted ways in the yard, my lord?"
The words came out sharp, and that, too, irritated
her. She ought to be grateful that he had brought
her so far in only a few hours. But she wished him
anywhere else just now.

Then he glanced at her, and she could not mistake
the faint amusement in his eyes, nor the concern.
That unsettled her. She did not want him being concerned for her. No, she did not.

Busying herself with dragging off her gloves and
undoing the ribbons to her bonnet, she heard his
boots on the floor, and then the creak of the chair
next to her as he sat down.

"Miss Colbert—Audrey, it is highly improper of me
to pry, but I am going to. Why do you need to fly
north in this manner? I do wish you would trust me."

Brushing at the curls on her forehead, she glanced
up at him. He had taken off his hat, and his hair
looked rumpled, as if he had just dragged a hand
through it. Dust lay on the shoulders of his coat,
turning the blue pale, and she wondered if he could
be as thirsty and out of sorts as she. He did not look
so, but he had ordered them refreshments, after all.

Her displeasure faded. This must be nearly as frus-
trating for him as it was with her. If only he . . .

No, she would not wish for it. He loved Chloe. She
had seen how he looked at his intended. She would
not do anything to ruin that for him.

So what could she tell him?

Wetting her lips, she tried to compose her
thoughts.

Arncliffe waited. The advantages of his training, he
thought, mouth twisting. A lord often spent long

hours waiting. At court for his king's pleasure. At Parliament through dull speeches for vital votes. In endless reception lines at the social affairs that commanded his attendance. He had the schooling to wait for hours—and for her he could wait even longer.

He had glimpsed the hesitation in her eyes, and that brief flicker of wistful yearning, as if he had almost tempted her into sharing whatever burden lay on her. Then she looked down to smooth the soft kid of her gloves and he wondered if she would insist on pushing him away.

What a devilishly headstrong female.

But, of course, she must be the one who managed everything within her family—a rather heavy responsibility for such slender shoulders. Her father had died years ago, he knew. He had seen how little her mother could get about. And the past week had been a revelation about how little sense Chloe seemed to have, even though he kept telling himself that it must be wedding jitters that made him start to see her in another light. She seemed so different from the woman he had fallen in . . .

He stopped himself. His feelings did not matter now. Not when he had promised himself to Chloe. A gentleman's word could not be broken, and so it did not matter if Chloe now seemed not at all what he had thought her. A good lesson—even if learned too late—in the lack of wisdom in a speedy courtship. But he had thought himself finally to have been as lucky as his brother.

Well, no use brooding about it. He had another lady to think of at the moment.

"This is all such a disaster," she muttered.

She said nothing more and he wondered if he ought to press harder for answers, only guilt stung him for having already stepped so far over the bounds he had lived within all his life.

At last she seemed to make up her mind about something, for her gaze lifted to meet his. "I am embarrassed to admit this, but, well, I am running away. I am trying to catch up to the man I love. His name is Fitzjoy and he is an Irishman, and my Great-uncle Ivor would not consider a match between us. So Mr. Fitzjoy took himself away, but I am determined to catch up to him so we might marry."

And what I will tell him when we do catch up with Fitzjoy and Chloe is something I will have to deal with then, Audrey thought, holding her breath and waiting to see how Arncliffe would take this new tale.

His frown deepened. *He will never believe this,* she thought, desperation welling. But then he nodded and took her hand, his touch as gentle as if he held some priceless object. She let out her breath. *Oh, no, he does believe this of me.*

"No wonder you asked about an Irishman at the tollgates. Well, he must be a decent fellow if you hold him in such regard. I shall do all I can to help you. I did not wait all those years for love to appear in my life only to scorn another for such fancies. Now, just where is your Mr. Fitzjoy bound for?"

She stared at him, then stammered, "Scotland—I think."

"You think?"

"Well, I—that is, he did not tell me directly, other than to say he was leaving. And I—oh, bother, I have no idea what direction he went off in. I am only following a hunch."

Rising, Arncliffe paced away, one hand rubbing his chin. Then he turned. "Pardon me for a moment," he said and with that he let himself out of the room.

Audrey leaned back in her chair and rubbed the

spot between her eyebrows with two fingers. She had not known that inventing tales could be so taxing. Would she ever keep all of it straight? Her face burned. Oh, how could she tell such falsehoods?

But she knew how. She glanced at the doorway. She could do it for him—for his happiness. Straightening, she started to work out just what she might possibly do when they caught up to Fitzjoy. If they did.

The maid—a white apron over her blue muslin dress—knocked and then came in with a brass tray that held a pewter jar and mug, a glass, and a pottery pitcher. The lemonade and ale, Audrey assumed. She gave an absent thanks, and then kept worrying.

By the time Arncliffe returned, she still had no plan, only a growing sense of desperation, as if she had wound herself so tightly in sheets during a dream that she could no longer move.

Only that was silly.

To prove it so, she sat up and poured the drinks—kept cold in an icehouse before they had been brought, she assumed, or in the cellar—as Arncliffe outlined what he had done.

"I assume he is traveling by carriage, which means he must change horses, and if he is headed north he will most likely have changed somewhere between Barnet and Stevenage. At Barnet, I'd guess, for thirty miles with the same team would be a miracle unless he took the entire day. I've sent grooms from the inn to find some trace of his trail, so it won't be long until we're after him in earnest. For now, I suggest we have something to eat."

Audrey tried to smile at this. And when the roast chicken and pigeon pie and the peas in cream and strawberries arrived she tried to do more than pick at the meal. Good as it smelled, her stomach tightened on every bite. She now dreaded coming across Fitzjoy and Chloe.

To make it worse, Arncliffe asked about her romantic tale. She had to invent a first meeting, the instant attraction, the painful parting. Hoping to distract him from wanting more lies, she asked, "But you said that you had waited for years for love. Is that true?"

His cheeks reddened and he glanced away. Then he looked back and admitted, "It unmans me to own to such a sentiment, but perhaps I can regain some ground by telling you that I had an example to envy. My brother's. Or at least the wife he found himself. The titles came to me, but I've told Arthur often enough that I would change places with him in a moment." He grinned, and suddenly looked years younger. "Of course, he's not such a fool that he would."

"But you also found your ladylove," Audrey protested.

"Have I?" He pushed away his empty plate. "I thought so, and then—well, you know your cousin far better than I. Is it that . . . well, is she perhaps shy in my presence?"

"Chloe? Well, no. No, I do not believe so."

"Then why does she seem a different person from the one in her letters—from the one I fell in . . ."

A knock on the door interrupted, leaving Audrey wide-eyed and her insides knotted tighter than ever. Arncliffe came back, his expression polite as ever, but she noted the disappointment in his eyes. "Not a trace of him, I'm afraid. At least not towards Barnet. Are you certain he came north? Does it not seem likely that he might have sailed for Ireland, and so gone south or west to a port town?"

Audrey sat frozen. Sailed? She had not thought of that. Could Fitzjoy be taking Chloe to Ireland? However, English law held there, unlike in Scotland, where a girl did not need her guardian's consent, nor to be over twenty-one, to marry. But if not north, where else? The Isle of Man? No, that too lay to the northwest. The Channel Islands? That seemed a possibility, as well, for they held to their own laws.

She gave a sigh. The world suddenly seemed far too large to search for one particular Irishman and a stolen bride.

Glancing up at Arncliffe, she asked, "Do you think he might have sailed from London even?"

"Perhaps. Though he would have to wait for a ship's passage there. He's more like to find a regular ferry from Southampton or Liverpool." Arncliffe frowned. "In fact, I seem to recall—or was it him? No, I believe it was. It was certainly some Irishman talking to Whitaker about taking the loan of Whitaker's yacht to pay off a gambling debt, and I know Whitaker keeps the *Elegance* docked in Southampton."

Torn now, Audrey bit her lower lip. Did she give up her chase north? But what if this proved a mistake? What if Fitzjoy, expecting a chase, had not set out on the Great Road North, but on one of the smaller lanes? It seemed so little to go on. Yet what else did she have?

Arncliffe's hand covered hers, his touch warm, his wide palm and long fingers engulfing hers. "Trust me, will you? We'll gallop south, and if I don't find a trace of him on the way we'll at least be in London where I've staff who can scour the docks and every tollgate that leads from the city. I'll find him for you."

And that is exactly the problem, she thought, as she allowed him to help her to her feet. He probably could do just that. Heaven would certainly have to help her then.

He galloped the fresh team back to London, his

jaw set with concentration, but with a gleam in his eyes as if he found unholy pleasure in this mad dash. Even his hat sat at a more rakish angle than usual, and Audrey dared not distract him as he feathered past the mail coach and other vehicles, dashed through towns, and galloped up and down hills. Twice she squeezed her eyes shut, once as Arncliffe drove his team from the road and onto the verge to pass a lumbering stage loaded with passengers on the top seats. She bounced from her own seat as the carriage bumped over grass and rough ground and grabbed for his arm, and then shut her eyes, half expecting to hear the screech of wood on wood as the wheels of the two carriages caught.

Wind brushed her face, and then Arncliffe's low, rumbling voice made her open her eyes again. "So little faith? Well, you have my permission to clutch me as much as you like—I rather enjoy it."

Mortified, she let go of him and straightened, then glanced back at the stage they had passed.

At the next close brush—this time into the narrow streets on the outskirts of London—she gripped her hands together and closed her eyes. But the memory lingered of strong muscles under her hands, the brush of her shoulder against his, the pleasant warmth of his body with the wind cold on her cheeks.

She risked a glance at him now. London traffic— hand carts, wagons, carriages, riders, and pedestrians—had forced him to slow his sweating team to a trot. Somehow he found a path around every obstacle. His mouth curved slightly and that warm light danced in his green eyes so that they sparkled, bright as the water in a mossy river.

What had he been about to confess back at the inn, she wondered for the hundredth time? That he had fallen in love with Chloe? She knew he had. She had seen him do so on his first meeting with her, and he had even told her that he loved Chloe with all his heart. So why had he mentioned the letters? Chloe's letters.

Biting her lower lip, she sent up a silent prayer that what she now feared would not be proven true. But a treacherous part of her whispered the doubt— what if he had fallen in love with the writer of those letters?

But he was pledged to Chloe.

Oh, had she perhaps not done the right thing after all?

She shut her eyes tight once again, wishing that she would wake in her own bed to find this nightmare gone. Only the carriage swayed as Arncliffe wove through London streets and lanes, and she could smell the city with its odors of horse and coal fires and the faint fishy decay of the Thames, which had grown stronger in the warming days.

Opening her eyes, she pulled in a breath. Well, she would just have to sort things out once they found Fitzjoy and Chloe.

And she forced herself to push away the uncharitable desire that somehow she might avoid ever finding her cousin and that Irishman.

Smothering a yawn with her hand, Chloe sagged against Fitzjoy. She did not want to lean against him, but she was so tired of this hard-seated gig. With the sun bright and the day warm, she had pulled off her cloak and had bunched it under her, but even that did not help. Hunger growled in her stomach. And she thought that if she stood up now she would fall down, for her legs seemed as stiff as the leather underneath her.

"Can we not stop?" she pleaded. She had asked before. And she got the same answer as ever. A wicked grin. Only this time he also tucked his arm around her.

She stiffened. She ought to push him away. Or slap him. Or tell him to remove his touch from her person. Only his arm there made it so easy to snuggle against him. And she could shift her weight a little now to a more comfortable position.

"Please? I'm ever so famished."

He tightened his hold. "You won't die of missing a meal. That much I know."

"But I do not want to miss a meal. And I am parched beyond parched. Can we at least not stop for something cool to drink?"

Fitzjoy glanced at her, then at the sky. A few hours of daylight left yet. Thank God for summer. Then he looked at the placid gelding who seemed to have the endurance of Job, if not the speed his four legs ought to warrant. Well, perhaps a short stop would not go amiss. He could use a stretch of the legs himself.

At the next crossing of a river, he guided the gelding off the road and pulled it to a halt, having to haul hard on the reins to stop the beast from its perpetual steady walk. After setting the brake, he jumped down. Then he turned and held up his arms to lift Chloe down.

His hands closed on the soft curve of her waist. Such a slip of a thing, really, he thought as she leaned into his hold. He swung her down, enjoying it more than he should. Golden curls bobbed, and her dress rustled, releasing a flowery scent that mixed with the warm summer air around them. She took an unsteady step, so he tightened his hold on her again. Just to steady her. Nothing more. He didn't intend another kiss, but he found himself wanting one just the same.

She had a mouth made for tasting, lush and ripe and red. A mouth to tempt any man to his downfall. Ah, he'd have to watch that mouth of hers. And the rest of her as well, or she'd have him losing his wits. But Tyrone Michael Fitzjoy never did that. No, he was a man wise to the world. A man with ambitions. A man who needed only the funds for the scope of his vision.

And she would give him that. She and her tidy fortune. And her lack of male relatives to come after him. Oh, there was some uncle or other, but not much of a guardian really. He'd asked after her background well enough. The old fellow never left his club, for all anyone knew, and she had only that lame old lady and that tall cousin of hers to care about. Thank God the money came with Chloe, not that cousin with her aristocratic nose that she looked down at the world from. He had sworn to do anything to make his fortune, but he would rather tame this pigeon than that female hawk of a cousin of hers.

She seemed to steady on her feet, but she did not move away. Instead, she gazed up at him from under dark, long, sooty lashes and smiled. "Thank you."

Warning danced along his skin, but the blaze she kindled elsewhere in him took his mind. He had seen her give other men that arch look, and he had ground his teeth when she had done so. But while he hoped to be no fool for her tricks, he had to admit they heated his blood just fine.

Taking a reluctant step away from the temptation of her, he swept a bow. "You've only to wish for water and here you are."

Blue eyes dancing, she gave him a mock curtsy,

then turned and strolled to the river. He watched her, taking pleasure in the sway of lush hips under the brocade skirts. He grinned. A fine shepherdess she made, like something from that grand French queen's court.

Frowning at himself, he turned away and strode to the gelding's head. Undoing the check rein so the horse could graze, he muttered to himself, "It's not your head you need to hold onto, lad. Just keep thinking of the money. You want her wed right and tight so all that money's yours." And then he glanced towards the river. Ah, but what harm was there in stealing another kiss or two before he bound her and her fortune to him?

With a grin, he set off to the river.

He found her standing on the bank, her mouth pulled into a pout. She turned to him at once. "I have no cup."

He thought about telling her that she had two hands. Or that she could—like any Irish lass—lean down and drink straight from the rapid shallows. It certainly wouldn't hurt her to humble that stiff neck of hers a bit.

Only the pleading in her eyes and that childlike note of distress dug under his defenses.

With a shake of his head, he turned. It took but a moment to find a tree with broad enough leaves. He broke off the widest leaf he could find, shaped it into a funnel, and knelt by the river, an odd stirring inside him. When had he ever gone to so much trouble for a woman?

Jaysus, but she could almost make him feel a ruddy knight, not some Irish knave.

Leaning out over the bubbling water, he cupped the leaf into the river, aware of her watching his movements.

The shove came hard and fast as Chloe pushed him into the river.

As he thrashed in the shallows, Chloe turned, picked up her skirts, and ran for the gig. With luck, he would drown. Or at least be slowed enough for her to slip away. And it would serve him right to have to walk soaking wet to the next village. She smiled.

But then she heard his curses. She ran faster, her legs pumping hard and her breath shallow and fast.

The gelding started as she ran for him, but he only took a step away before stopping again. Then she had hold of the gig's railing and was pulling herself up into the seat. She would make her escape, and then she would see this ruffian punished. Yes, she would.

She had almost gotten herself into the seat of the gig when a wet arm wrapped around her waist.

CHAPTER SIX

Kicking back, she tried to hold on to the gig. Her slipper came off, and he dragged her from the carriage as easily as he had plucked that leaf from the tree. She squirmed in his hold, but then he thumped her onto the ground. Spinning around on one foot, she flailed at him with fists but he grabbed her wrists, dragging them behind her, pulling her sharp against him.

Breathing hard, she glared at him, but the hot flame in his black eyes stopped her from doing more.

He looked more than angry. His black eyebrows rode low over his dark eyes, and that wide, sensual mouth pulled into a hard line. Her heart thumped harder as she stared at him. His black hair, dry in front but dripping behind, clung to his neck. His wet clothes pressed against her stomach and thighs; however, the heat from his chest and arms seared through her. She could see the pulse beat livid and fast in his temples.

Perhaps she ought not to have pushed him into the water.

"I—I—" she stuttered, unwilling to apologize, but thinking she somehow ought to explain.

He shook her. "One more word and it's walking

you'll be—back to London, and left by yourself! D'you hear me?"

Her eyes widening, she could only nod.

"You're a spoilt girl, you are. And why it's you haunting m'dreams instead of that nice Miss Parker with her ten thousand a year, I'll—"

"I haunt your dreams?"

"Like a bloody succubus."

She frowned. "Just what is that? It does not sound at all nice!"

"It's a witch. A demon of a female—that's what you are!"

"Well, I suppose that is a bit better than it sounded."

Fitzjoy shook her again, furious with her now. "Better? I'll tell you what would have been better— my never laying eyes on you. Or hearing that you'd money. Or that I'd never need come to this god-forsaken land. Better would be my having more than a ruin of a house and five sisters to think of— not that I'm marrying you for any of them, mind. I've a taste for fine living, I have. I like having enough to eat as well—and having more than enough to drink. And silk sheets suit me far better than linen. It's for them that I'm marrying you. Not for some crumbling ruin that would eat through your riches faster than famine can starve a man."

With a last shake, he pushed her away. She stumbled on her hem and sat down hard on the ground. Tears started to her eyes. She seemed to struggle with them a moment, and then burst out in sobs, her words half choked, "No one ever wants me!"

"Ah, sweet saints in heaven," Fitzjoy muttered, not knowing if it was a curse or a prayer, and wondering what he did now with this plague of an heiress.

* * *

The news did not cheer him. Arncliffe glanced at the young groom who stood before him, cap clutched in his hands. The fellow's chest had puffed with pride at having been first back—and within the hour. Arncliffe had promised a guinea for any news, and double that if brought at once. Only he had not expected this.

Folding his hands behind his back, Arncliffe smiled anyway. He could think of more questions, but none this lad could answer, so he only said, "Thank you, John. Smollet will see to your reward. And please ask him to call the others back. Oh, and is a fresh team at the ready as I asked?"

"Yes, m'lord. And thank you, m'lord." With a bow, the groom took himself off, and Arncliffe turned and strode through his town house to the back garden.

He had brought Audrey to Arncliffe House, for he could think of nowhere else for her to wait as he organized the hunt for word of Fitzjoy. He certainly did not want to leave her at some public inn, and she could not go home—although she ought to now, he thought. The groom had been quite specific about what the gatekeeper at the crossroads for the New Kent Road and the London Road had said of the woman traveling with Fitzjoy.

A right pretty piece.

The gatekeeper had remembered the Irishman, both for the early hour he had passed and the beauty of the lady with him. That description, however, seemed far too vulgar to fit any lady. Nor did it suit the possibility of a sister.

A right pretty piece.

Arncliffe frowned. Perhaps Fitzjoy, having given up

hope for Miss Colbert, had sought consolation in other arms. Even so, that did not put Fitzjoy in the most pleasant of lights. What was Audrey doing conceiving a fancy for such an unsteady fellow?

A day ago he would have described her as a sensible woman, dependable and even tempered. The sort to make wise decisions. He had thought her kind and elegant, but with a dry sense of humor. Of course, two weeks ago he would have described his betrothed in much the same terms, but she had since made him wonder if he knew nothing of women. Perhaps that was the truth.

With a shake of his head, he let himself out of the house and strode into the garden, which had just begun to hint at the lush flowering of summer.

Audrey glanced up, then rose from where she had been sitting on a stone bench set in an arched wrought-iron arbor. For a moment he hesitated, his thoughts tangling suddenly like a schoolboy's. She had washed the dust from her face and had done something with her hair, piling it loosely instead of pulling it back in a tight knot. That wretched bonnet was gone, and the late afternoon light pulled a soft nimbus from her hair, finding touches of gold in the brown. The light also outlined long, shapely legs within the thin muslin of her gown and shift.

Arncliffe's mouth went dry.

He had never seen her this way before, and jumbled thoughts of ancient pagan priestesses or goddesses flitted past, what with that proud carriage of hers and the lush foliage around her, and . . .

And what was he doing entertaining such notions when he was engaged to another? Had he not just condemned Fitzjoy for such fickle behavior?

She came forward, her expression anxious as she asked, "You have word?"

To make amends for his gaping at her, he tucked her hand into the crook of his arm and started with her to the front of the house, keeping his eyes fixed on his steps and not on her. "Southampton it must be. His carriage passed by the tollgate at the Elephant and Castle in the early hours on the road southwest. I doubt we'll cover the distance in anything less than eight or nine hours, but if you care to leave now, we've a few hours of daylight and a full moon tonight."

"Yes, please, do let us leave at once."

He stopped in the hallway and then turned to her. He dared not say anything of the woman traveling with Fitzjoy—what if his suspicions were wrong and she was *Miss* Fitzjoy? Still, he had to give Audrey some warning of what they might discover at the end of this quest.

"Miss Colbert—Audrey, I . . . well, I am going to pry again. Are you certain you wish to do this? Having committed myself to another, I think I can speak from experience when I caution you to rethink your passion while you can. The heart can choose so unwisely."

She looked away, her cheeks as pink as the rosebuds in his garden. "Do we ever really have a choice in such matters, or is it something that happens to us? Something beyond our control—falling is perhaps an apt description. An unavoidable trip and fall. We are drawn to someone because of some attribute, some element of beauty or grace, some quirk of personality, and then, quite out of our control, the heart tangles on deeper feelings and is caught."

He still held her hand, he realized, for her fingers trembled within his. Fearing to break the intimacy between them, he kept his voice soft as he said, "But perhaps one trips and falls less often if one does not have one's head in the clouds?"

She looked up at him, her gaze now steady, her

eyes endlessly deep. Her lips curved in a faint smile. "But how dull to be a plodding person who is too careful and too safe. I'd rather have my passions misspent than face a life spent without love."

"Even if that love should prove to be in vain?"

"Oh, there is always a lesson to be learned, a gift waiting to be discovered even in the most heart-wrenching of loves—and so how could that prove worthless? No, the sadness, I believe, is only to find oneself incapable of love. Now that would be an empty life. But we are wasting time, my l—Connor."

Her smile widened as she said his name and the urge swept over him to simply pick her up, carry her out to his coach, and take her away with him. A ridiculous idea, really. The Marquess of Arncliffe could never do such a thing. Not when he had promised himself to another. And when her feelings were engaged elsewhere. Only he found himself entranced by her words, by her low, throaty voice, by the hint of passion in her tone—entranced and wondering why he had spent so much more time with her dazzling cousin rather than with this quietly attractive lady.

Life had to get better after this, Chloe decided, glancing about her as moonlight filtered into the barn.

Not so much a barn, she decided. More a ruin. And not even a romantic ruin of an abbey or a castle. Just some stone walls, the faint smell of cow, musty straw, and a thatched roof that showed glimpses of stars and rising moon.

She sighed—only Fitzjoy was not near to hear her. Or was he?

After her tears had spent themselves, he had

helped her to her feet, tossed her into the gig, and then climbed up beside her and said not a word more. She had thought a few times about saying something, only each time she glanced at his face, his expression made her think that perhaps she really ought to keep quiet. He did not look a man who could be pushed any farther.

Mouth tight, eyes dark, he had kept the gig to country lanes, skirting past villages and avoiding the main roads. Dust had made Chloe sneeze, but she said nothing. She had sat with her hands folded, sniffling occasionally and giving deep sighs, but he had never asked about these.

At some point, she must have fallen asleep, for she woke to find it dark and to find herself being carried in Fitzjoy's arms. She had stirred, but then he had laid her onto something softer than hard ground. A faint musty odor drifted to her, but she only wrinkled her nose and snuggled into soft fabric, drifting off again.

Hunger had awakened her. She sat up to find herself on a bed of straw, her cloak laid over it to keep the shafts from poking her. Moonlight streamed into the barn—or what looked like a barn to her, what with the gelding dozing in a corner of the structure and wide doors open to show the gig in the yard of what looked a ruined farmhouse.

There had not been a sign of Fitzjoy.

She shivered now and thought about pulling her cloak around her, but what would she sit on then? Besides, summer warmed the air around her. Night birds of some sort sang, and she could hear animals rustling in the surrounding woods.

She could leave now, she supposed, but where would she go? She had no idea of their location, really. She ought to have paid more heed to their direction. But even if she knew more, she did not care to wander about the countryside at night.

Her stomach growled and she put a hand over it.

Then a soft voice drifted to her, startling her. "Is it a lion you keep tucked inside you?"

She relaxed, relieved to have company—even his company—and to hear the pleasant lightness back in his voice. However, she forced a frown. She really could not display her happiness at having him return.

And then she caught the scent of roasted chicken.

"Food! Oh, you wonderful man! I vow I *would* eat a lion if you had brought me one."

With a flash of white teeth, he sat down beside her. Shadows obscured his face, but he must have seen her pale hands, for he took one and then placed a cloth in it. She fumbled with the bundle, finding half a roasted chicken tied inside.

She glanced up at the dark shadow next to her. "Do you not have a plate? And I shall need a fork and knife, please. And something to drink—I would prefer wine rather than lemonade."

For a moment, he did not answer. And then he gave a low chuckle. "So would I, dear one. But what you have is what's in your hands. And if you're too much a lady to eat with your fingers, I'll be glad enough to finish it for you."

She glared at him, then realized he could not see her doing so. And the bird really did smell delicious. "Well, I suppose if you can do no better than this, I shall have to make do!" She bit into the chicken. Warm juices dribbled down her chin. She wiped them with her fingers, then settled into eating.

"Do no better?" he said after a moment, his tone aggrieved. "That's not much gratitude."

Swallowing a mouthful of chicken, she said, scorn

in her voice, "Yes, I suppose I ought to be grateful you rescued me from a marriage to the Marquess of Arncliffe. How awful that would have been, to be obliged to be a great lady!"

He gave a laugh. "And that's to wound me, is it now? The thought of you married to a stuffy lord—as if you'd ever be happy with that."

"He is not stuffy. He is . . . dignified."

"A veritable boring paragon of virtue. And what would you be wanting with that? Him and his lot are things of the past, or they will be soon enough. Their kind thinks a man's birth or the cut of his coat means something more than what's in his head or what he can do with his hands! They don't even see the revolutions changing the world around 'em, and not just the political ones, mind. There's fortunes to be made with new industries and new inventions. It's the men of The City—the bankers, the merchants, the ones putting in manufactories and backing clever inventions—"

"Such as that steam carriage in London which exploded a few years ago?"

"That one failed. And perhaps the next will. But some clever fellow, he'll get it right—if he hasn't already. And that's the fellow I'll back with my money."

"You mean my money."

His grin flashed. "Yes, your money. But think on it—what would you rather be? A marchioness, married to a dull fellow, weighed down by a chain of traditions, suffocated by a world that tells you what you can and cannot do? Or one of the new leaders—the real ones, with the freedom to make your own rules? With a husband who's making you so rich that even those old biddies will come round to smiling at you and inviting you to all their affairs?"

Chloe stared at him. She wished she could see his

face better. Did he really think that a title meant so little? The passion in his voice seemed deeply felt, and it stirred an answering excitement. How much fun to be a setter of fashion—to be someone who remade the world. Oh, it would be risky. Failure would mean ruin and ostracism. But had he not already dragged her outside Society's boundaries?

She frowned.

Of course, all this was bound to sound alluring, what with moonlight streaming into the barn and that soft accent of his making his words sound smooth as the finest silk.

Bundling up the chicken bones in the cloth, she wiped her fingers as best she could on it, then pushed it back at him. "You sound quite mad, you know!"

His grin flashed again, and moonlight threw dim light on his profile. Her heart tightened as his words flowed over her. "Ah, but it's a fine madness that stirs the blood—like that of a long, hot kiss that sears you through to your soul."

Her face burning and her mind empty, she turned away and wished she had some clever, sharp answer for him. Audrey would have had something to say. She had nothing. And the thought of her cousin made her think of her aunt. Tears stung her eyes again. Why had she not listened to them? Why had she not been a dutiful girl?

She lay down on her cloak again, though she doubted she would find any rest.

She would have to tell him the truth. That's all there was to it. She ought not to have lied, really. She winced at the stories she had told him. Well, perhaps somehow she could gloss over the fact that Chloe had gone willingly with Fitzjoy to something as vulgar as a masquerade. And perhaps he would be angry with her, not with Chloe for seeking out Fitzjoy's attentions.

Taking a breath, Audrey twisted in her seat to face Arncliffe.

He had had a team of six horses set to his traveling chaise, and the closed coach—after a day already spent in his open phaeton—seemed luxury. Soft velvet cushions covered the seat and seat backs. Matching burgundy velvet drapes could be pulled over the glass windows. Roses had been set into the crystal holders beside the door, giving a faint perfume to the coach, and the lanterns outside the doors offered a pleasant warm glow.

They had stopped every ten miles to change horses. "We will make the best time with frequent changes," he explained. At two of the stops, he had confirmed sightings of a dark-haired Irishman who matched Fitzjoy's description. However, for the past three stops, they had not had word of such a person.

Now, Audrey studied Arncliffe and wondered how best to disclose the truth.

He sat with his legs stretched out before him in the spacious coach. He had tossed his hat onto the seat that faced backward, and had sat, arms crossed, in companionable silence. Oddly, she had felt no urge to babble in the intimacy of the coach. And he seemed to feel no need as well to make conversation.

But they must talk now—for they would need to start asking after not just Fitzjoy, but an Irishman who might be traveling with a young lady.

Taking a breath, Audrey let it out slowly. Then she hurried into the truth before she could think better of it. "I . . . my lord, I have a confession to make. I . . . I have not been completely honest. I am not following Mr. Fitzjoy because I care for him, but because he has abducted Chloe and I was afraid to confess this to you."

Staring at him, she waited for his answer.

CHAPTER SEVEN

For a moment she heard only the beat of galloping hooves on the hard, dry summer road, and the creak of the carriage springs. Then the softest of snores reached her. The carriage rounded a bend and the lantern light from outside the coach fell briefly across Arncliffe's face.

Eyes closed, face relaxed, he stirred as the light drifted across his features, casting the rugged masculine contours into rough peaks and valleys, making him more startlingly handsome than ever. He did not waken. The road straightened, and the dim gloom of the carriage hid his features from her again.

Still, she continued to stare at him. Did she not know already every line of him—the straight nose, that sharp edge of his jaw, the curve of his cheek? Her mouth twisted. Here she was, disclosing her sins to a sleeping gentleman. She turned away to stare outside the window on her side of the coach, at countryside made into ink etches by the silver moonlight. Then she looked back at him.

He must be exhausted to fall asleep in this fashion. After all, while she had rested at his house, he had been busy arranging matters. He stirred again as the moonlight slanted into the coach. She glanced at it, her mouth pulled down. Rising and steadying herself against the sway of the coach by bracing one hand against the back seat, she reached across him to pull closed the curtain. The coach gave a lurch and she fell back into her seat, landing next to him, so close that her breasts brushed his arm now.

He stirred and she thought he might wake, but he only shifted, turning so that his head fell onto her shoulder and his hand came around her waist.

Muscles tensed, she held herself still. What now? Wake him? Push him away?

His breathing deepened back into steady, rhythmic pulls.

Experimenting, she pulled one arm from his hold and then tried to shift his weight. He mumbled something, and he did shift, but only to snuggle closer, so that his face now rested low on her shoulder and just above the swell of her breast. With a contented sigh, he seemed to slip into deeper sleep.

Desperate, heart thudding, she wet her lips and glanced about her. But no one was here to see her predicament. No one would know.

Lifting one hand, she bit down on the tips of her glove and drew it off. Then she brushed her fingertips across his forehead. He did not move. Growing bold, she brushed her lips across the spot where her fingers had touched. He tasted warm and sweet. She pulled in a breath, intoxicated with him.

Longing swept through her, sharp, fierce, bright as the summer sun. Now that she had him in her arms—solid and real, and no longer a recollected story from Chloe—she knew that she had lied to everyone, herself included.

She never really had intended him for Chloe. No, she had used her cousin shamefully. She had lived through her cousin, counting each success of her cousin's as her own. She had chosen Chloe's gowns, and selected the events for Chloe to attend. She had guided Chloe into her engagement to Arncliffe, and had convinced herself that it was because it was such a perfect match. She had told Chloe what to say. She had even written Chloe's notes to Arncliffe.

And she had told herself it would be enough to see him happy with Chloe, to see him settled with such a beautiful woman—a woman he loved. She had thought she could live as the indulgent second cousin to their children.

But the longing ache inside mocked such intentions with the truth—she loved him. And it was not enough to give him to Chloe and watch him marry her cousin. But it would have to be so. He had given his word. And he was a gentleman.

Shifting herself, she settled her arms about him, making him and herself more comfortable. And then she laid her cheek against the softness of his hair.

The carriage rocked as the horses galloped into the night. For another night she would keep lying. She would imagine herself to be as pretty as Chloe, to be as rich, and to be eloping with the man she loved, a gentleman accustomed to beauty and to having the best of the world.

And, come the morrow, she would stop the deceit. He might well be happy then to turn his back on the entire Colbert family. But she would be greedy tonight and keep him in her arms.

He woke with a stiff neck, shivering cold, to find his heiress gone. Jumping up, Fitzjoy glanced around the barn, seeing only the gelding, placid in its stall, and a black velvet cloak on the ground. He took it up

and her scent swirled around him—lavender and
rose. With a muffled curse, he strode to the door.
Now what would he do? And what did she think herself doing, jaunting around on her own where any
sort of devilment might befall her?

He scowled at that. Perhaps she thought the worst
had already happened—but he had not touched her.
No, he'd wait for a proper ring on her finger first
and all the legalities tied up for them in Guernsey,
where a man might marry with as few ties as could be
had in Scotland.

However, there were half-pay English soldiers back
from the war with little to do other than make mis-
chief, and they'd not be so kind to such a beauty.

Muttering curses, he wondered why he had ever
thought her lack of male relatives an advantage. Now
he knew it for the disaster it was. She had never
learned to mind anyone, least of all a man.

Well, time she learned.

Striding to the gelding, he threw on the beast's bridle and buckled it into place. With his luck, the nag
would probably not be broken to saddle and would
throw him, but the hunt for his heiress would be
faster on horseback.

He led the horse from the barn and then stopped
at the sight before him.

She sat cross-legged in a patch of wild daisies, her
skirt billowing around her, her shoes—pretty, dainty
things fashioned with low heels after those of the last
century—next to her. Even in her rumpled brocade
overskirt, her curls tumbled loose, she looked fresh
as the dawn itself.

His irritation sharpened. What was she doing giving him such a start?

Still frowning, he dropped the reins, leaving the

gelding to graze, and strode to her. "And what do you think you might be doing here all on your own?"

She glanced up, her expression calm. His heart seemed to stop for an instant. Mother Mary, but she was a beauty, with that spun-gold hair and that heart-shaped face and those wide, wide blue eyes. She looked like the dawn, right enough, all pink and golden and soft blues.

"I am resigning myself," she said.

"Resigning now, is it?"

"To marriage with you. We have spent the night together—however chaste."

His frown deepened. "It's not rape I'm after."

"No, you made it quite clear you want my fortune, not my person. Therefore, I shall marry you, for my reputation is in ruins if I do not. You may then have my money and I shall go to a nunnery."

He couldn't stop the grin. "A nunnery? You'd be trying to take the veil as Christ's bride, would you? You'd not be an hour in any cloister before you caused so much trouble they'd want you packed and gone from their hallowed halls."

Her chin came up. For a moment, the blue eyes sparkled. Then she turned to pick a daisy. "I do not expect to become a nun, merely to seek refuge from an unkind world."

He almost laughed at such melodrama, but the tremor in her voice checked his mockery and he stopped grinning.

Throwing himself in the grass beside her, he plucked the daisy from her fingers. "Just how has this world ever been unkind to you? You're an heiress— the most courted lady in London. That's not sounding too unkind to my ears."

She glanced at him, hot scorn in her eyes. "What would you know of it?"

Shrugging, he twirled the daisy. "What would I not know—I'm an Irishman in England."

Tilting her head, she studied him. Then she blurted out, "The other girls hated me in school—they always said such horrid things about me. And then my parents died . . ." She looked away, and added, her voice soft, "They called me an orphan, as if that was something awful. And then, when I went to live with my aunt and cousin—well, I tried to make them like me. I did. But I could tell they did so only from duty."

"And don't you know why?"

She shook her head.

"Dear one, have you never looked in a mirror before? Another woman would have to be a saint to look at you and not be jealous—and then it's themselves they don't like, first for not being so blindingly beautiful, and then you for making them feel catty about it. Men lust for you, and women hate you for it, and it won't ever leave you much company, save for those who'll stay by you long enough to see there's a person under that face of yours."

"What do you know of anything?"

He grinned. "Oh, I know jealousy. I'm Irish, dear one. And it's jealous English hands that have been trying to take our land from us for well over the last seven hundred years. It's a land you'd love—all willful beauty like yourself. Lush and seductive. It's no wonder you English keep wanting it.

"And I know what it's like to feel alone—so alone you'd swear you could die and not have it matter to anyone. There's plenty around London who'll make an Irishman feel unwelcome. But what matters is this."

He took her hand in his. "This matters—skin to warm skin. Human touch. Reaching out to another even if they slap you away for it."

Uncertainty clouded her eyes. Then she looked at him and said, her voice small, "I only want to have others like me—I thought they would if I were a marchioness."

Smiling, he touched her cheek with the daisy, trailing the petals over her skin. "Then start by liking yourself more. And if that fails you, it's my eyes you can look into to see just how much someone does care for you."

With a sigh, she leaned against him. "I should love that."

He grinned, tucked the daisy into her hair, then stood up and brushed his hands. "Good, now if it's resigned you are, would you care to resign yourself to a hot meal? There's an inn not a quarter mile down the road in Chawton."

She stared up at him, and then her eyes narrowed. "An inn—a quarter mile away? And you allowed me to sleep on the ground!"

He grinned and started to stroll back to collect the gelding. "Seems as if we're even, then, for that swim I took yesterday."

"Oh, you—you . . ." Reaching down, she picked up her shoe and threw it at his back. The slipper bounced off his broad shoulders. He glanced back at her. "You might be wanting to hang onto those a bit—no reputable inn I know will feed a woman who arrives looking a barefoot harlot."

The slowing pace of the carriage woke him. For a moment he lay still, his thoughts and dreams tangling in a pleasant lassitude. What had he been dreaming? Something about Chloe writing to him? No, it had been Audrey, only instead of her sitting at her desk, she had been in a garden, dressed in something white and transparent as she wrote on a scroll in her lap.

He had watched her scribbling as if from a distance, and then in one of those shifts of a dream, he stood next to her, watching her write down the same words she had spoken to him in the garden.

But you told me that already, he had said in the dream.

She looked up at him, then stood and faced him, the gown around her pulled tight against her figure to show the slender waist, the pert breasts that would fit so nicely into his hands, the slim curve of her hip. *No, I haven't told you anything.*

And then she spun in a circle, changing into Chloe as she laughed at him and danced away, spinning from Chloe to Audrey to Chloe to Audrey. Chasing her, he caught her, dragging her into his arms—only now he could not recall whom he had caught. Chloe or Audrey?

He frowned at that scrap of dream now, unsettled by it, and to his body's response to the dream-woman pressed against him.

Then, as awareness woke in him of the slender form next to him, he realized that at least part of his dream had a basis in reality. Somehow Audrey had ended up with her head on his chest and her body reclining against his. The faintest recollection stirred of his almost waking last night, of finding himself wrapped in her softness, and of pulling her closer as he leaned into the corner of the coach and drifted to sleep again.

No wonder his dreams had been so delightful—and so vivid.

As a gentleman—and one betrothed to another lady—he could not consciously allow the situation to continue. Only Audrey looked so sweetly comfortable.

Sleep softened her mouth and the dawn light played over her face, pulling attractive angles from the high cheekbones and the strong nose. He wanted to run a finger down the slight bow outward of that nose—a nose of character and determination.

Reluctant, but unable to put it off any longer, he gently pushed her from him, settling her in the opposite corner of the carriage. Then he leaned back in his own corner and said, his tone brisk, "Good morning, Miss Colbert. I trust you slept well."

She sat up at once, one hand to her forehead, a dazed look in her eyes. He smiled at her. He hoped the formal use of her name might ease the situation, putting them back on familiar, distant ground again. Only she still looked tousled, her brown hair softly disordered and her eyes wide and dark. He could not help the thought: *I should like to see her every morning like this.*

Immediately, he looked away.

The carriage had slowed enough that he could take a measure of their location. He let down the window. Not Southampton yet. No salt tang to the air, no cry from sea birds.

He glanced back at Audrey. She had smoothed her gown and put on her bonnet again. Nothing could take the creases from her dress, but she had her face well starched again.

"Would you care to take breakfast while the horses are changed?" he asked. "We have made such good time that I think we could afford a short rest."

With a small incline of her head, she said, "Thank you. But before we stop, I must have a word with you. There is something I have not told you."

An echo of his dream tickled the back of his mind. He pushed it aside. "Of course. However, I do insist that you have that word with a hot cup of tea in your hands. No, no argument. Look, we have stopped already. Come now, let me help you down."

The footmen had opened the door. Arncliffe jumped down, but rather than wait for the footmen to let down the steps, he reached into the coach, caught Audrey by the waist as she stood in the carriage doorway, and lifted her down.

The action surprised a slight smile from her. He smiled as well, and then she looked up at him, her smile fading, those brown eyes of hers widening.

The images from the dream teased him again.

"I caught you just so last night," he said.

Something sparked between them. He felt it in the current that drew him to her.

And then a startled voice interrupted. "Audrey? Is that you? Whatever are you doing here with Arncliffe?"

Guilt stung, Arncliffe spun on his heel to find his intended bride standing in the yard just outside the inn, staring at him and her cousin.

CHAPTER EIGHT

Seeing Chloe, Audrey broke from Arncliffe and ran to embrace her cousin. "Chloe, dearest—we found you!" She hugged Chloe again, then held her away. "You are a wretch!"

Chloe had been clutching Audrey's arms, but now she stiffened. "I am? I am not the one standing in a stable yard making eyes at another lady's husband to be!"

"Oh, that—Connor was just helping me from the carriage."

Chloe glanced from Audrey to Arncliffe. "Connor, is it?"

And then Fitzjoy stepped from the inn and strolled forward, "Connor who, dear one? Is it friends you've met?"

Dropping her cousin's hands, Audrey turned to the Irishman, her temper simmering. "Why you . . . you scoundrel!"

His stare ran up and down her. Then his black eyebrows lifted. "Ah, not friends. Relations. Come to wish us happy, have you?"

Audrey raised her hand to slap him. Then everything seemed to happen at once. She swung. Fitzjoy caught her arm. He jerked her off balance, and then Fitzjoy lay sprawled on the ground, an astonished expression on his face. Arncliffe stood beside her, his fists clenched.

In a rustle of skirts, Chloe hurried to Fitzjoy, shooting a cold glance at Arncliffe as she swept past him to kneel beside Fitzjoy. "You brute!" She dropped down beside Fitzjoy, heedless that he lay in the yard of an inn. "Are you hurt?"

With a growl, Fitzjoy started to rise.

Audrey stepped between the gentlemen, too aware of the attention they had drawn. One of the grooms had called out, "A mill! My money's on the gent who's handy with his fives!" Another took odds for the dark Irishman. Mortification to be in such a public scene scalded Audrey's face.

Through clenched teeth, she muttered, "Shall we take this inside—please?"

Nursing his jaw, Fitzjoy allowed Chloe to help him rise. "I suppose a man whose bride I've stolen away is allowed one swipe at me—but only one, mind. The next comes at a cost."

"Stolen?" Arncliffe repeated, brows snapping together and lifting his chin so that he stared down that elegant straight nose of his at Fitzjoy.

Audrey watched him, her heart beating sick and fast in her throat. Arncliffe's expression seemed an utter mask of icy aristocratic arrogance, and she would not blame him if fury raged under that now daunting exterior.

Then Chloe said, "I am not going anywhere." She sounded absurdly petulant.

Audrey took her arm and started for the inn. "Not now, Chloe. And certainly not here."

The innkeeper looked dubiously at her when Audrey asked for a private parlor, but when Arncliffe stepped forward to demand attention to the lady's request, the fellow jumped. Audrey sighed. How lovely to have someone leap to obey one so well.

She led Chloe into the parlor shown to them at the back of the inn. Her cousin at once shook off her touch and went to stand beside the unlit hearth, her arms crossed and her chin high. But Audrey caught the glitter of uncertainty and fear in Chloe's eyes. She reminded herself that the events had been a trial for Chloe as well.

Fitzjoy strolled in, looking insolent and yet with a defensive air to him not unlike Chloe's. He did not stand next to Chloe, but positioned himself in a stance that looked to Audrey as if he expected more fisticuffs. She rubbed her forehead. Perhaps she *ought* to allow the gentlemen to brawl over Chloe like two farmers for a prize heifer.

Arncliffe came into the room, glanced around, then turned and ordered ale, tea, and coffee. He held out a chair for Audrey and swept Chloe a bow, saying, "Shall we at least be comfortable? I have the distinct feeling this requires considerable, lengthy explanations.

He sounded so controlled, so delightfully civilized that Audrey wished she could kiss him. She settled instead for giving him the unpolished truth. "Fitzjoy ran off with Chloe."

"He did not!" Chloe said, arms dropping to her side. "I went with him to a masquerade, and then we took a long drive."

"Oh, please! We have told enough lies—both of us." Audrey turned to Arncliffe. What had seemed possible in the dark intimacy of a coach now loomed as an impossible task. She took a breath and dived into it, however. "I have not been truthful. I was not running away to elope with Fitzjoy."

"With me? I should hope not—you've not the . . ."

"Careful, sir," Arncliffe warned, fixing the man with a glare. "I will not have Miss Colbert insulted."

"I am not insulted—yet," Chloe said.

A knock on the door interrupted, and a maid came in, bearing coffee, tea, and ale on a tray. The warm aromas mixed and tantalized, but with refreshments poured and the maid gone, Audrey found herself unable to swallow even a sip of tea.

Arncliffe poured himself a mug of ale. He hesitated a moment, then poured one for Fitzjoy. "Now, as to explanations—shall I save everyone's breath and tell you what I gather to be the facts? Chloe, I assume from your actions this morning that you would prefer to release me from our betrothal, since you seem to have contracted another understanding."

"Well, I—" Chloe glanced at Fitzjoy.

Fitzjoy stepped forward, black eyebrows flat and a bruise swelling on his jaw. "You can't marry him—you know you can't."

Chloe twisted her hands together. "But I said I would."

Arncliffe glanced from one to the other. Even he could see the invisible tug of something between them. The fellow really ought to be made to suffer for his crime. On the other hand, his abduction of Chloe had prevented Arncliffe's marriage to the girl. That had to count for something.

Perhaps Chloe might well be the making of the man—and he of her. Arncliffe decided to hope for that. And if the two had been on the road overnight—as had he and Audrey—then something had to be done to make all this respectable.

Putting down his tankard, Arncliffe walked over to Chloe and took her hand. "Miss Colbert, you made me a happy man when you accepted my offer. You will make me even happier if you release me from it. However, should you wish it, I shall honor my word, marry you, and see this fellow treated to the full prosecution the law allows."

He heard Fitzjoy's sharp intake of breath. He could feel Audrey's stare on his back. He kept his gaze on Chloe. She looked a child suddenly—uncertain and afraid. He leaned closer to her. "It really is all right if you don't love me."

"Really? Well, I suppose if you do not mind terribly. But I should have liked very much being a marchioness."

"Thank you. But that probably is not sufficient reason to wed." He turned to Fitzjoy and as he approached, the Irishman stiffened, his feet shifting to a fighting stance.

Amused, Arncliffe smiled. No one had ever thought him so threatening. "No need for that. So long as I hear nothing but wonderful things from Chloe about her life, I shall not feel obliged to defend her."

"As if it would be anything to you."

"I intend to make it something to me. Now, I suggest a return to London. I shall procure a special license, and a bishop, for you. It shall be a small wedding—just family." He glanced at Chloe, then leaned closer to Fitzjoy. "And I suggest you ask her properly now if you want a sunny face to see you back to London. A garden is vital. Moonlight would be better, but if you go down on one knee and kiss her senseless, you might survive the next day or so without sulks."

Fitzjoy frowned. Arncliffe nodded to the door, and the Irishman grinned suddenly. "Ah, now I see why it's an interest you're taking. Well now, I could do with a relative such as yourself." With a wink to Arncliffe, he went to Chloe. "Come, dear one, there's a garden I must show you, it seems."

"Oh, but why can I not stay here—I vow you are always dragging me someplace. And if we are now to be married in London, I want a proper wedding dress, and flowers, and . . ."

What else she wanted fell away as Arncliffe shut the door on them. Then he turned to Audrey, who sat on the edge of her chair, back straight, eyes solemn.

"You ought to know the full truth—I wrote Chloe's letters to you. I pushed your match with her." She looked down at her hands. "You must think me the most managing of females, trying to trap you into a marriage with my cousin."

He came to stand in front of her. "Yes, you are clever enough that you nearly did. Your cousin certainly dazzled me with her looks, but it was those letters . . . charming, funny, warm letters . . . that captured my heart."

She looked up at him. "I do beg your pardon. I should not have meddled, but I . . ."

"Please, I cannot talk to you with me standing over you in this fashion—either you must stand, or, no, I have a better idea." He went down on one knee.

She took his hands and tugged, trying to make him rise. "Please do not. I should be the one to kneel to you to beg for your forgiveness."

"For what? For too many stories? For giving me the most adventure I have ever had, and the most fun? Ever since I proposed to your cousin, I suspected something was not right. Only I did not know what to do."

With a soft moan, she turned away. He took her chin in his hand and turned her face to his. "It took meeting up with you, driving up and down the countryside, listening to your outlandish stories, to realize that you wrote those letters. Those wonderful letters.

I realized it last night. My dream finally showed me what I think I must always have known on some level. And I can only thank God that my engagement to the wrong woman is ended so that I can court the right one."

She stared at him. "The right one? How can I be right for you when I am not pretty, or rich, or . . ."

"Marry me." He took her hands in his.

"But I deceived you!"

"Yes, and while I hope you do not make it a habit, we shall have to do a bit more of it in London—do you think anyone will believe if we say the newspapers made an error and printed the wrong Miss Colbert's name? It sounds a bit thin, but then I am so respectable that enough may swallow the story to make it stick."

"Oh, but I . . . I . . ."

"I thought you did not want to turn away from love, no matter what the risk."

"I don't—but I cannot think that I deserve this."

He stood and pulled her to her feet. "I tried, as your cousin would approve, on bended knee—let me now try my way. Marry me!" He did not wait for an answer, but pulled her into his arms. His hands closed tight around her waist, and his mouth covered hers. She fit him as if he had bespoke an order for her. For a moment, she held herself still, and fear fluttered through him. Would she, like her cousin, find him wanting?

A fierce possessiveness flared inside him. He would not allow that. Tightening his hold, he forgot his fears, forgot his title, forgot everything except the press of her lips to his, the touch of his tongue to hers, the warmth of her, the sweetness. She softened into him and he deepened the kiss.

Finally, breathless, his heart pounding, he came up

for air. She stood in his arms, her face flushed, her breath rapid and shallow. He smiled as he saw the pulse fluttering in her throat—and then he kissed that hollow on her neck.

"Please—I cannot think when you do that," she said.

"Must you think?" he asked, his words muffled. "Just tell me yes—tell me that you will wake up beside me each morning. That you will write me absurd, darling letters. Tell me that you love me as much as I adore you."

"Yes—I love you. And I do not deserve this—but I am not such a fool as to say no to you. But what are we to tell everyone? The wedding invitations have gone out. The date is set. St. George's in Hanover Square has been reserved!"

He smiled. "My dear, I have every faith you shall think of an excellent story by the time we reach London. But until then I have other plans." And with that he settled to lay full claim to her attention.

A PERFECT DUET

JENNIFER MALIN

CHAPTER ONE

"For half my life I begged my father to take the family into London each spring," Miranda Granville said, stepping out of the milliner's shop. "Isn't it curious that after three Seasons, I'm delighted to be staying in Gladstone this year?"

"Are you?" Her longtime friend Lady Elizabeth Ellsworth squinted as they moved into the sun. Adjusting her bonnet, she said, "Now that Edmund and I are betrothed, I know he should be my whole world, but I confess I rather miss the social whirl of the city."

"You were always better suited to the social whirl than I." Miranda glanced up and down the village street before they crossed to the shady side. "But surely planning your wedding must be more exciting than attending a few balls and routs."

The bride-to-be sighed. "Frankly, my mother has taken charge of all the planning. I have nothing to do but buy clothes for my trousseau."

Miranda laughed. "Such a sad lot in life."

A village woman selling flowers from a cart called out to them as they passed. "Flowers for my ladies? First roses of the season."

"How lovely." Lady Elizabeth stepped up and selected two nosegays of white roses. She passed one to

Miranda and lifted the other to her own nose. "Perhaps you're right about spending this spring in the country. In London, the flowers never quite smell this lush, I think."

The vendor grinned. "There's no place like Gladstone in the spring, my lady. No other village in Cumbria can rival our May Day festival."

"I had forgotten about May Day." Elizabeth handed the woman several coins and turned to Miranda. "We must attend the May Day festivities."

A twinge of uneasiness wound through her. Miranda didn't like large gatherings of any sort. The only time she felt comfortable among a crowd was when she played the pianoforte. Somehow, the music made her forget her insecurities. "Do you think so? It's been such a long time."

Elizabeth took her arm, and they set off toward Ellsworth Manor again. "All the more reason to go."

Miranda held up her nosegay and sniffed. "Who do you suppose will be chosen May Queen?"

"You will, doubtlessly."

"Oh, surely not!" She dropped her friend's arm, the mere thought heating her cheeks. "No one ever takes note of me."

Elizabeth grinned. "With Letitia Osgood married and my wedding pending, you are hands down the most marriageable female in the village. Everyone is aware of that."

"And that's a good thing? Only one person needs to be aware of it—and, frankly, he doesn't seem to be taking note."

Her friend took her arm again. "Actually, this could be the perfect chance for you to bring my brother up to scratch. Julian will likely be crowned May King, and the two of you can spend the whole day dancing and making merry together. 'Tis just the sort of occasion to inspire him to make a public declaration of your . . . arrangement."

Since Miranda's childhood, her family and the Ellsworths had intended her and Lord Julian for one another, but now she was nearly two-and-twenty and no formal announcement had yet been made. Her first Season out, she'd been in no hurry to marry. The following year, her grandfather's death had put her in mourning. Then last spring, Julian's grandmother had died. This year, however, no impediments remained, and he still hadn't spoken. The situation was on the verge of embarrassing her.

She cast her gaze downward as they turned onto a path that cut through a stand of woods nearing the Manor. "Julian leads such a carefree life as a bachelor that I begin to doubt he'll ever settle down."

"Oh, he has every intention of marrying you," Elizabeth said. "The only trouble is that he feels no urgency, while you, as a woman, can't wait forever. Somehow we must convince him that the wedded bliss you can offer him will be far more exciting than his current state."

"I fear I don't strike people as a very exciting woman. At gatherings, most people don't even notice me."

"Except when you play the pianoforte," Elizabeth said. "Everyone's enthralled by your playing."

"Not quite *everyone*. And though Julian professes his admiration, my music hasn't persuaded him that life with me would be heavenly."

"I fear he isn't exactly an aficionado. His pursuits are less serious." Elizabeth tapped her chin with a finger. "To impress him, you'll need to do something a bit daring. You need to show him you're not the mouse he thinks you are."

"I am the mouse he thinks I am."

"No, my dear, you are not. You can be quite lively when you're among people you trust. You mentioned that you're happy to be staying in Gladstone this year. Take advantage of your ease here and make an effort to come out of your shell."

She took a deep breath. "I suppose I could try, but I'm not certain how I'll fare. Sometimes I wish I were more like you, Eliza."

Elizabeth stared off into the trees in thought. "We need to come up with a plan to show you in your best light. Give me time, and I'll think of something."

Miranda kept quiet, but she'd begun to doubt anything would work with Julian—short of asking her father to intercede, which she would never do. Though technically the match was arranged, she had always hoped that Julian really loved her. She still recalled the time at his sister's sixth-birthday party when a maid had offered him and her a choice of red or white lollies. He'd chosen red for both of them and, as the servant left, had said to Miranda, "Red is for love."

Never had a ten-year-old said something so debonair.

Does he mean that he's in love with me? she had wondered at the time, awestruck.

Since then, however, he'd taken many other opportunities to flirt, but her question remained unanswered.

As she and Elizabeth emerged from the woods, the faint notes of a pianoforte drifted out of the manor house. Miranda recognized a strain of Beethoven's *Für Elise,* superbly executed. Something coiled inside her abdomen. Only one person of her acquaintance—besides herself—could manage that piece with proficiency.

"Mr. Owen is visiting?" she asked her friend.

"Yes. He arrived yesterday." Elizabeth scanned her face, then rolled her eyes. "I don't know why you let his comments bother you, Miranda."

The knot in her midsection tightened. No one stole her composure like Andrew Owen. She didn't know why, either. Well, perhaps she did—it was because he was always right! Normally when she played, she lost herself, completely fluid, completely confident. Mr. Owen made her doubt her competence, made her see that as far as she had come, she still wasn't quite at one with the music.

"Why does he have to focus so intently on my playing?" she asked. "Why can't he just leave me alone?"

"Your playing is hard to ignore, and music is Andrew's life. I swear he only means to help you, but doesn't treat the matter with enough delicacy. He's told me dozens of times how much he admires your playing."

"Yet criticism is all he has for me."

"Not when he speaks to me about you." Elizabeth turned onto a walk that led around the side of the house. "Julian's probably with him now. Let's go to the conservatory."

"Must we?"

"You ought to say hello to both of them. 'Tis only civil."

She sighed. "Very well, but I'm not going to play, no matter what Mr. Owen says. He always insists I play."

"Doesn't that prove he enjoys your music?"

Of course it didn't, but Miranda didn't answer, the growing sound of the music drawing her attention away. As they approached the vicinity of the conservatory, the tumbling piano notes grew stronger and came more rapidly.

Entranced by the building arpeggio, she slowed her pace.

Through one of the large windows, she spotted Mr. Owen at the keyboard, his movements vivid, his shock of blond hair flicking about as he struck the keys.

As she watched his fingers fly, her heart pounded. The instrument was an extension of his being. He didn't need to think about what key to strike any more than he had to remember to breathe.

Spellbound, she glided toward him, and the strains of the music swelled to exquisite heights. Throughout her body, her muscles contracted until she nearly couldn't bear the tension. Just as Elizabeth opened the French doors leading to the conservatory, he pounded out the climax of the movement.

Miranda sucked in her breath.

Cascades of softening notes rolled over each other to close out the song. He caressed the keys with the final notes, and gooseflesh rose on her forearms and thighs.

By God, he plays like . . . like a sorcerer, she thought.

A moment of awed silence followed. Then Elizabeth burst into applause, striding into the center of the room. "Bravo, Andrew! Bravo."

Mr. Owen turned around and gave the newcomers a crooked grin. He met Miranda's gaze, and a lump formed in her throat. Even a simple look from him could rattle her.

"Cousin Eliza and Miss Granville. What a pleasant surprise." He got up to meet them, his smile dazzling. His white teeth and blue eyes complemented the golden aura of his hair. He bowed to Elizabeth, then took Miranda's hand and bent over it. As he let her fingers slide from his, she shuddered, obviously still suffering the effects of his playing.

"The Beethoven was magic," she breathed.

He lowered his gaze but smiled again. "Thank you, Miss Granville. Coming from you, such an assessment means much."

"Hello, Miranda," another male voice intoned from the opposite corner of the room.

Her gaze flew to Lord Julian, who rose slowly from an armchair. The object of her long-term *tendre* was a darker version of his cousin. His features were less angular than Mr. Owen's, and his hair and eyes were tinged dark brown. He epitomized the phrase "tall, dark, and handsome."

He gave the ladies a perfunctory bow without coming forward. Reseating himself, he picked up a magazine and leafed through it.

"I was hoping you'd stop by, Miss Granville," Mr. Owen said. "Tell me, does my technique seem at all improved to you?"

"I believe so." Oddly, her voice still sounded breathless. The man truly flustered her. "You must be doing something different."

"Yes, I've been trying to maintain a balance of tension and relaxation throughout my arms and shoulders while I play. I hope we'll have a chance to discuss it. For the last few months, I've had the pleasure of studying with David Desroches."

The name of the renowned pianist nearly made her gape. She looked at him more closely. "Monsieur Desroches is in England—and you have been studying with him?"

"He has given me a few lessons." He grinned again. "I've mentioned you to him."

Skepticism shot through her, at last breaking the spell of his music. How dare he tease her about a matter she took so seriously? She crossed her arms over her chest. "I find it unlikely that Monsieur has time to chat about unknown and virtually untrained female musicians."

"*Au contraire.* Being French, Desroches is always interested in the fair sex. He was delighted to hear that England's premier female pianist is also a beauty."

"Oh, *please.*" She turned away. Grabbing her friend's arm, she tugged her toward the door to the hall. "Come on, Eliza. Let's show your mother the hat you purchased."

Elizabeth looked back over her shoulder and shrugged. "She doesn't believe you, Cuz."

Miranda's face burned as she exited. Why did Mr. Owen always have to toy with her? *England's premier female pianist,* indeed. She knew a sarcastic remark when she heard one.

Andrew frowned as he watched Miss Granville go, her coppery curls bouncing. She held her head high, affording him an excellent view of her delicately curved neck.

Why did she never take him at his word?

"Tsk, tsk." His cousin stepped up behind him. "Heavy-handed compliments don't work with Miranda, Cuz. You'll need more finesse to impress a woman like her."

He glanced over his shoulder with a curled lip. "And I suppose you have more finesse?"

Privately, however, he knew Julian was right. Miranda Granville was sensitive, and Andrew didn't seem to have the savoir faire to address her properly. He could no sooner pay her a compliment without offending her than he could offer her musical advice.

"I've had Miranda pegged since she and I were in the nursery," Julian said. "Goes to show you that I've always had a way with females."

"A title will warrant you that." Andrew tried to smile, but he couldn't quite keep the bite from his tone—not that he really resented his cousin's title. His own prospects were good enough, and the female interest he gained through his musical skills usually made up for what he lost in having no title.

Except when it comes to Miranda. The thing he did resent about Julian was that he had Miranda—and for all Andrew could tell, he didn't even want her.

"Speaking of ladies," Julian said, "let's walk over to the Red Lion and have an ale. There's a new barmaid working there—Betsy. I want to remind her to meet me at the bonfire on May Eve."

Andrew crossed his arms over his chest. He almost wished Miranda were still standing outside the door to overhear. Would that have cured her of her *tendre* for his cousin? Or, after all these years, was she so resolved to marry the rogue that she'd accept him even if she knew all of his failings?

Julian grabbed his jacket from the back of a chair and slung it over his shoulder. "Are you coming with me or not?"

Andrew wasn't keen to go, but only that morning he'd promised his uncle he'd try to temper his cousin's drinking. How he was going to do so, he had no idea. "I'll come, but can we keep it to one pint? I'd like you to go shooting with me this afternoon, and we'd do better with clear heads."

Julian shrugged. "Very well. Your besting me on the range *has* become tiresome. One pint it is."

One the way out, they stopped by the front hall to fetch hats. The sound of feminine voices drifted out of the drawing room. Andrew glanced through the door and saw Eliza and Miranda on the sofa without his aunt.

Julian moved to the threshold of the room. "I thought you two went to show Mother your fribbles."

"She is occupied with Cook." Eliza picked up a copy of a fashion periodical and flipped through the pages. "Where are you and Andrew going?"

"To the Red Lion to hear what the villagers have in store for May Eve. It's been years since I've attended a bonfire. The efforts of other towns always pale in comparison to Gladstone's. Somehow we've managed to retain the pagan spirit of the old Beltane customs here."

"May Eve, you say?" His sister lowered her magazine. She gave Miss Granville a sideways glance, then looked back to her brother. "Why, Miranda was just telling me she wants to attend the bonfire this year."

Andrew could scarcely believe his ears. The local May Eve celebrations often ended with inebriated couples slipping off into the woods for a tumble. Of course, a well-bred female wouldn't know that, being shielded from such activities. He brushed past Julian. "Pardon me, Miss Granville, but you don't want to attend the bonfire. It's sure to degenerate into a sordid occasion."

She lifted her chin. "Is that so?"

Julian followed him into the room, smirking. "No doubt Miranda intends to be safely home in bed by the time the festivities grow raucous."

"No, no," Elizabeth said. She glanced toward the doorway, apparently to check for eavesdroppers. In a whisper, she continued, "Miranda means to steal out of her house just before midnight and be present for the best part of the evening."

Miss Granville looked at her friend with raised eyebrows, and Andrew wondered if she were being goaded into the adventure. It wouldn't be the first time his fair cousin had led her astray.

He shook his head. "Out of the question. The risk of being accosted is too great. Everyone present will be drinking."

Julian grinned. "She'll be fine, Cuz. I'll wait outside the gate at Granville Lodge and accompany her to the bonfire myself. 'Tis a brilliant scheme. It will be the most amusement we've had in ages, Miranda."

Just like Julian to encourage such a daft plan. And with the way he drank, he couldn't be counted on to protect a lady. Andrew grimaced. "I'll go with you, then."

"Hardly." His cousin waved a hand at him. "You'll only spoil the fun with that Friday face of yours."

It was all Andrew could do not to roll his eyes. He had no intention of leaving Miss Granville to his cousin's care, but there was no sense arguing with him. If he had to, he'd follow Julian to make sure nothing untoward happened.

He slapped his hat on his head. "Are we going to the pub, or have you changed your mind, now that you and Miss Granville have plans for May Eve?"

"No, I still have business at the pub." He turned toward the ladies and gave them an exaggerated bow, his spirits obviously boosted by the foolhardy scheme. "Miranda, I'll meet you outside the gates of your house at eleven on Friday night."

She gave him a wavering smile and nodded. "Thank you. I look forward to it."

Andrew bowed, too, and swept out of the room. Without waiting to see if Julian followed, he strode out of the house and turned onto the path that led toward the village.

Every visit to his relatives' got more vexing. At one time, when he was seven or eight, his audacious, slightly older cousin had seemed daring and funny. Then they'd reached their teens, and Andrew began to notice Miss Granville. At first he viewed her merely as a competitor for Julian's attention. Then her musical talent began to emerge, and his ears perked up. She was the only other young person he knew who could play Beethoven as well as he. He thrived on the competition between them, and at some point his admiration for her grew physical as well as musical. Unfortunately, her infatuation with his cousin lingered. She'd never given him reason for hope.

The sound of quick footsteps swelled from behind him. As he reached a bridge that spanned a small stream, Julian joined him. "What's the hurry, Cuz?"

He ignored the question. "How are you going to handle the barmaid now that you've made arrangements to meet Miss Granville on May Eve?"

"Why? Are you hoping I'll leave the barmaid for you?"

Andrew snorted. "If I want a loose woman on May Eve, I'm sure there will be plenty on hand at the bonfire."

His cousin laughed. "True enough. Some wench there is likely to take a fancy to you—but I didn't think the bonfire would be your cup of tea. You'll attend then?"

He kicked a stone off the dirt path. "I'll be there."

"The Beltane magic must be strong this year. Even the wallflowers are determined to enjoy themselves. Imagine both you and Miranda joining the festivities."

Andrew looked at him with a frown. "You do realize you'll have to treat Miss Granville differently from the way you handle your barmaid consorts? You can't lure her into the bushes and have a tumble with her."

"Dear Cuz, you forget, Miranda and I are practically betrothed."

His jaw dropped. "You don't mean to take her before you put a ring on her finger?"

Julian laughed. He bent and scooped up a piece of fallen branch from the road, breaking twigs off the main shoot. "Don't look so panicked. Miranda would never allow that, though it may be interesting to see how much she *will* allow. Do you know I've never even tried to kiss her?"

Actually, Andrew had wondered about it. Gazing off into the shady undergrowth beside the trail, he enjoyed a brief sense of satisfaction, knowing they'd never kissed. Then he remembered that May Eve would likely change the situation. He cleared his throat. "What will you tell the barmaid when we reach the Red Lion?"

"I'll tell her to meet me at midnight."

"You can't make assignations with two women for the same event!"

"Of course I can." Finished stripping his branch, Julian used it as a walking stick. "Didn't you notice that I fixed on eleven o'clock as the time I shall meet Miranda? *She* won't want to stay out long. We'll walk to the bonfire, spend a half hour there, and have a mug or two of mead. Then she'll complain of the noise or the insects, and I'll take her home. Naturally, I'll show her a 'short cut' through the woods, so I can try my luck with her on the way."

Andrew grit his teeth. "And what if the barmaid shows up at the bonfire early?"

"It won't happen. The Red Lion doesn't shut until eleven, and she'll have to clean up afterward."

He shook his head. "You have no scruples."

"Come on, Cuz. Are you telling me that if you had

two beautiful women seeking your company on the same night, you would disappoint one of them?"

They emerged from the woods, stepping onto the start of Market Street in the village.

After the shade of the dense trees, Andrew squinted in the sunlight. "Better that than risk disappointing both, if they find out about one another."

"Perhaps *you* might disappoint two women, even if they didn't know about one another." Julian laughed and put his hand on Andrew's shoulder. "I'm jesting, of course. But rest assured, I shall disappoint no one on May Eve. I quite look forward to the evening."

They reached the tavern and Andrew shrugged off his cousin's grasp, reaching for the door handle. *This may be my last visit to Gladstone,* he thought. He didn't know how much more of Julian he could bear. The May Eve scheme gave him a sense of foreboding. Either the barmaid would show up early, or Julian would drink too much and compromise Miranda.

He could almost hope for the former, if it wouldn't mean Miranda would be humiliated. As for the other possibility, perhaps he could prevent it if he kept an eye on the pair.

Entering the pub, he bit his lower lip. He didn't relish the prospect of attending the bonfire and watching his cousin try to steal kisses from Miranda. He would go, however, and make damned well sure that Julian pressed his luck no further than that.

CHAPTER TWO

On May Eve, Miranda could barely follow conversation at dinner, let alone eat. Her thoughts raced with anticipation of her rendezvous with Julian. She wondered if he would try kissing her tonight . . . at last.

She would let him, too. Frankly, she was ripe for the experience. Elizabeth had had her first kiss years ago, flirting with one of the stable boys right here at the Lodge. Miranda had never even held a man's hand. What would a man's lips feel like on hers?

"You've barely touched your mutton, dear," her mother said, snapping her back to the present. "Are you feeling under the weather?"

She blinked. "Actually, my appetite *is* rather off. Perhaps if I retired early, a good night's sleep might help."

"She *must* be unwell," her father said, a hint of sarcasm in his tone. "I've never known Miranda to go to bed early. She's more likely to play pianoforte until midnight, keeping the entire household awake."

"I'm sure I'll be fine in the morning." Miranda felt a twinge of guilt about lying to her parents, but at this point she had no choice. If she didn't bring Julian to the sticking point soon, she'd end up a laughingstock as well as a spinster. She had no recourse but to go through with the scheme Eliza had suggested.

"Go on then," her father said. "You don't look peaked to me, but if you're fatigued, you should rest. You're excused."

"Thank you, sir." She rose and left the room, careful to slow her steps so she wouldn't look too lively.

Inside her bedchamber, she changed into her nightgown. Likely both her maid and mother would look in on her before they retired. Sitting down on the bed, she checked the pocket watch she kept on the night table. Half-past eight—almost three hours to go! *Unbearable.*

She climbed under the covers and lay on her back, staring up at the ceiling. Her sense of guilt lingered, but excitement overshadowed it. She wasn't willing to forgo this plan. Sometimes one had to take a risk.

After a wait that felt interminable, her maid arrived. Miranda dismissed her. She tried reading a novel but could barely resist getting up and pacing. Finally, her mother visited and felt her forehead.

"Your cheeks are flushed, dear," she said, "but you don't feel overly warm. Does your head ache?"

"No, I'm only a little tired." Miranda grimaced at having to prevaricate.

Fortunately, once reassured that Miranda didn't have a raging fever, her mother didn't stay long, either.

Miranda listened to her footsteps fade in the hallway. When all went silent, she scrambled out of bed. Her watch read half-past ten. *Thank heaven!* She couldn't bear waiting a minute longer.

She slid into her most low-cut gown, a short-sleeved muslin with lace trim. If she was going to be daring, she might as well go all out. Throwing a shawl around her shoulders, she paused to listen at her door. All stood quiet.

As she tiptoed to her window, her knees nearly gave way. She hoped she wouldn't swoon, but she took heart in the fact that she had no history of fainting.

A balcony wrapped around the side of the house past her chamber, so slipping out would be easy. Poking her head through the window, she looked in both directions and saw no sign of movement. The sky was clear, and the half moon provided a fair amount of light. She stepped over the sill and scurried to the half wall guarding the edge. Climbing over it and down the trellis looked dangerous, but she reminded herself that she'd done it before, in her tomboy days.

She made her way down slowly, a cool breeze slapping her skirt about her legs. Once on the ground, she dashed across the garden and hid amongst a stand of trees. From there, she walked toward the gate, her heart pounding. An owl hooted above her, and she jumped.

What a goose I am, she thought.

She quickened her pace, trying to ignore shadows dancing in the darkness under the bushes and hedges she passed.

When she reached the top of the drive, Julian wasn't there. She felt for her pocket watch, but found she'd forgotten to bring it. Surely, it was eleven or later by now.

Her shoulders slumped. Julian wasn't known for his reliability. He'd been late on many occasions and sometimes even neglected events entirely. The sudden heaviness of her body made her realize how disappointed she'd be if he didn't come. She was so tired of waiting for him.

Sitting down on a large, flat rock, she pressed her fingers to her temples. Perhaps the time had come to acknowledge that he would never marry her.

The thought frightened her. Julian had always been in her life. What would she do without him? She'd never even attempted to appeal to other suitors, and at her age, whom was she likely to attract? Would her father even allow her to look for someone else, or would he insist that Julian marry her against his will? She didn't want a husband who'd been forced to take her.

The sound of gravel crunching made her look up to see a familiar male figure approaching.

She leaped to her feet. "Julian!"

"No, it's Andrew," Mr. Owen said just as he moved close enough for her to distinguish his pale hair in the moonlight.

A lump formed in her throat. Surprisingly, though, she felt more relief than anything else. Perhaps she hadn't really expected *anyone* to show up.

He stepped up beside her and frowned. "Isn't he here yet? It's quarter-past eleven."

She moistened her lips. "No, he hasn't been here. Haven't you seen him?"

"He hasn't been home since noon." He kicked a stone out of the road. Looking back in the direction he'd come from, he put his hands on his hips. No one else was in sight, and the only sounds came from chirping crickets. Sighing, he turned back to Miranda. "I hate to say it, but he may not show up at all."

She looked downward. Standing alone in the dark with Andrew Owen seemed shockingly intimate. She wasn't as well acquainted with him as with his cousin. "I know."

"It may be for the best." His tone softened. "You're better off staying home tonight."

She bristled. How annoying that even here he would try to tell her what to do.

"I'm not going home." She met his gaze. Her own words surprised her, but she realized she meant what she'd said. If she went home to bed, she might as well give up on Julian—and the life she'd always envisioned for herself. "I'm going to the bonfire."

Before he could object, she started walking up the road.

After an instant of hesitation, Mr. Owen ran up beside her. "I don't think he'll come to the bonfire, either. Frankly, if he does, he'll likely be in a state you don't want to witness."

A muscle in her cheek twitched. She knew Julian would be drinking and that alcohol didn't put him in his best form. But she didn't want to go home— maybe not ever—because it would mean the end of all hope. "Nonetheless, I want to attend the festivities."

They continued walking without speaking. She sensed him watching her and kept her focus straight ahead, refusing to acknowledge his stare of disapproval. As they approached a footpath that cut through the woods, he let out a heavy sigh.

"Let's turn here," he said quietly. "It's shorter, and among the trees, none of your father's friends will drive by and spot you."

She looked at him, astonished that he'd stopped protesting. His jaw was taut, and she thought he truly appeared concerned. His objections weren't meant merely to thwart her will, she realized. Privately she conceded that the crowd at the bonfire might be as dodgy as he predicted. She was grateful that she didn't have to arrive alone.

"Good point." She turned into the woods.

The crickets grew louder, and the visibility dimmer. Luckily they were both familiar with the path, though she found it strange to be there in the middle of the night, especially alone with him. Not another soul on earth knew they were there. Why, if he'd wanted to test her virtue . . .

But, of course, he had no interest in that. A tingle shivered down her spine, and she stumbled on a root in the path.

He moved closer and took her arm. "Hold onto me. It's dark."

She wasn't overly worried about stumbling again, but the warmth of his body felt reassuring. Due to the darkness and the narrowness of the path, they held each other closer than walking partners normally did. It occurred to her she'd never been so close to a man, other than the few times she'd waltzed, and that had been in a room full of onlookers. Again, the situation here felt exceedingly intimate.

What would she do if *Mr. Owen* tried to kiss her tonight?

She felt her cheeks heat, but she wasn't sure it was embarrassment that caused her to flush. She knew he wouldn't kiss her, and she almost felt . . . wistful. Would she never be kissed? Never hold a man's hand in any way but platonically? Goodness, but she was pathetic.

The faint sounds of cheers in the distance made her look up. In the distance, a yellow light glowed atop a hill.

"There's the bonfire," Mr. Owen said.

"Yes." She smiled faintly to herself. Julian would

likely not be present, but it felt good to do something daring for her own sake.

As they emerged from the woods and climbed toward the high flames, the sounds of shouts and laughter got louder. Feminine squeals of delight mixed with strains of simple music played on drums and a fiddle. Silhouettes of dancers and bystanders came into view.

When they reached the top of the hill, the fire crackled, and heat fanned Miranda's face. She looked at Mr. Owen, and he gave her a soft smile—not his usual lopsided grin. He seemed different tonight, more pensive. Evidently he regretted that his cousin had forsaken her. She had to admit that Andrew showed more responsibility than Julian. No doubt she was safer here with him than she would have been with his cousin.

She returned his smile. "Thank you for escorting me."

"I should have taken you home." He looked away from her.

The comment seemed more obligatory than threatening, so she ignored it. Scanning their surroundings, she said, "They're selling mead on the other side of the hill. Shall we get a couple of mugs?"

He hesitated, then shrugged. "Why not?"

Now that they were amidst a crowd, they loosened their grasp on one another, but she continued to hold his arm. Glancing around, she could see he'd been right about the drinking, and clearly more men than women were present. Judging by their dress, they were all villagers, none of them gentry. She'd grown up in Gladstone and didn't feel threatened, but she was glad that any interested party would see she had an escort.

Mr. Owen paid the barman and handed her one of two large mugs, overflowing with frothy liquid.

She took a sip and laughed in surprise, wiping foam from her upper lip. "It tastes rather like champagne."

"Yes. I quite like mead." He downed a mouthful, then guided her back toward the bonfire.

"Miss?" a feminine voice addressed her from a group sitting on a fallen tree trunk. "Aren't you the lady who bought white roses from me the other day?"

She recognized the flower vendor from the village. "That was my friend. Good evening, Ma'am."

"Have a seat." The woman pressed closer to a man who had his arm around her shoulders. "There's room enough here for you and your gentleman friend."

The spot she indicated appeared more suited to hold one, but it seemed impolite to decline. "Thank you."

Sitting down, she expected Mr. Owen would choose to stand, but he squeezed onto the log beside her. The warmth of his thigh pressed against hers penetrated her skirt and petticoat in a startling but pleasant way. Looking away from him, she took a swig of mead. It tasted even better than champagne, she thought.

"'Tis midnight!" a man shouted from the other side of the bonfire.

A cheer went up, along with a smattering of ringing bells and rolling drums.

The couple beside her sank into an embrace, lips locked.

Miranda's mouth fell open. Never had she seen such a display. She darted a wide-eyed look at Mr. Owen.

He laughed and held his mug up in a toasting

gesture. "To the May Queen, whoever she is this year."

She couldn't help glancing back at the others. They were still kissing. The oddity of the scene struck her as amusing. Turning around to Mr. Owen, she giggled and clinked her mug to his, drinking again.

After another moment the flower vendor emerged from the clinch and grinned at them.

"Why aren't you two kissing? A kiss at midnight on May Eve brings luck all summer." She looked at Mr. Owen. "Go on, Guv'ner, before it's too late."

Startled, Miranda glanced at him to gauge his reaction.

To her surprise, he bent toward her. Surely he wasn't going to kiss her . . .

But he did.

His lips were unexpectedly soft and cool with mead. Who would have thought Andrew Owen would taste of champagne and smell faintly of some subtle exotic spice? She closed her eyes and enjoyed the dizzy excitement that rushed through her.

"That's more like it," the flower vendor said behind her.

Mr. Owen backed away and winked at Miranda. "I feel luckier already."

She put two fingers over her mouth. Despite herself, she couldn't quite suppress a grin.

So do I, she thought, amazed.

She had to look away from him to try to conceal how giddy she felt. Gazing into the bonfire, she couldn't even pretend to take offense at his initiative. In the span of a few seconds, her long wait for her first kiss had ended—and in such a pleasing way. If all had gone as expected and Julian had been the one to kiss her tonight, she had no doubt she would have been fraught with anxiety. She would have spent the night worrying whether or not it meant he would finally marry her.

As it was, she knew that Andrew had kissed her only in the spirit of the moment. The experience had been simple . . . and nothing but enjoyable. Odd, because it should have happened with Julian. She should have been upset.

Somehow she was glad—and she had no desire to question her feelings, either.

Andrew looked into his drink, grinning to himself. He'd kissed Miranda, and she'd responded damned well. Knowing her arrangement with his cousin, he wouldn't have been surprised if she'd slapped him. But she hadn't. Lord, her lips were sweet. Julian was an idiot.

The thought of his cousin prompted him to survey the party goers on hilltop once more. Still no sight of him. Quite likely he and the barmaid had gotten together early and were off somewhere having a tumble. Andrew only hoped they remained where they were.

He glanced at Miranda again. She stared into the fire, a Mona Lisa smile on her lips.

Taking a sip of mead, he wondered for the hundredth time whether he should try to talk her into going home, but he had never succeeded in persuading her to do *anything*. Tonight he wouldn't bother to try.

He finished his drink and nudged her with his elbow. "Would you like to dance?"

Her brows rose. Then she nodded. "I'd love to."

She left her half mug of mead with the woman beside her. Andrew led her into the midst of four or five other couples enjoying a somewhat haphazard country reel.

In the past they had danced on a few rare occasions, but she had always felt rather rigid and awkward in his arms. Now she felt pliant and fell into step with him perfectly. He gazed into her eyes, and she smiled back before looking downward.

He bent to whisper in her ear, and she didn't recoil. "Not exactly like listening to Bach's *Piano Concerto Number Five*, but it will do."

She laughed. "Yes. Curious that of all works, you should mention that one. 'Tis one of my favorites."

"Rather a bittersweet piece to choose as a favorite."

"Perhaps." She tilted her head to one side. "But a thread of hope does wind through it, I think. I play it whenever I want to escape my life."

"Not often, then, I trust."

Her smile wavered. She looked past him toward the fire. "I've no urge to play it tonight, and that's all that matters at the moment."

She's unhappy, he thought. Considering how Julian treated her, the news shouldn't have surprised him. For years, he'd steamed over his cousin's neglect of her, but her feelings about it hadn't been clear to him.

Acting on impulse, he wrapped his arm around her waist and whirled her past another couple. She giggled, following his exaggerated dance moves with ease. As the song wound down, they collapsed in laughter.

He kept his arm around her as he escorted her back to the log. She allowed him the intimacy. Was he dreaming?

Afraid of pushing his luck, he finally let go of her when they reached their seats. Leaving her in the company of the flower vendor and her partner, he went and bought another round of mead for all four in the party. For some time afterward, he and Miranda sat enjoying the fire and making casual observations about the sights and sounds of the gathering.

When they'd finished their second drinks, she gave him a serious look. "Do you have a pocket watch with you?"

He sighed, reluctant for the outing to end. Tonight had been amazing, but what would remain of it in the light of day . . . with Julian in the picture? He pulled out his watch and flicked it open. "Half past two."

She blinked. "That late? I'd better start home."

"At this time of night, another hour or so won't make much difference," he couldn't resist pointing out.

"You tempt me—but then I imagine my father deciding to get out of bed and look in on me in my chamber." She grimaced. "I led my parents to believe I was retiring early because I felt under the weather. If Papa found my bed empty, I hate to think what his reaction would be."

"Hmm." He frowned. Her father had always had a foreboding air about him. "Is it like Sir Wilfred to look in on you when you're ill?"

"Not typical, but Fate has a way of choosing inopportune times for firsts."

"True." He stood and offered her his hand. She took it and rose as well. As they turned away from the now controlled fire, he entwined his fingers with hers. If he could walk through the woods holding her hand—and maybe steal another kiss before they parted—he would go to bed a happy man.

They inched their way down the hill.

As the clamor of the festivities faded behind them,

she glanced at him. "I don't know if it's the magic of
the ancient Beltane festival or just the excitement of
stealing out in the wee hours, but does this night
seem rather dreamlike to you?"

He hesitated. "Perhaps, but I prefer to believe in
its reality."

She looked back to the ground, sidestepping a tree
stump. "Why don't you and I usually get along this
well?"

"Perhaps we will from now on."

"I hope so. I believe I've always been rather intimidated by your musical expertise. Perhaps after this
experience I'll be able to relax around you. Then I
can concentrate better on what I have to learn from
you."

He shook his head. "I'm not qualified to teach
you. That reminds me, though: I meant to tell you
that I've written to Desroches about you. He has an
engagement in Penrith in August, and I've asked if
he'll consider visiting Gladstone to give you a few
lessons."

Her gaze snapped to meet his. Doubt flickered
across her features, but as she studied his face, her
expression transformed to one of astonishment. "Are
you serious?"

"Indeed I am. Don't let your modesty deceive you.
You're talented enough to study with the best mas-
ters. Your gender won't hinder you with Desroches,
either. Monsieur adores female students."

After a moment of stunned silence, she gave him
a little smile. "I don't know how to thank you."

"Wait until we see if he agrees to come. But I think
he will."

They were about to turn onto the path leading to
Granville Lodge, when the sound of twigs snapping
and underbrush crackling made them look up.

Julian staggered out of the woods, his hair disheveled and half his shirttail untucked from his breeches. He took a swig from a whiskey bottle and looked up, spotting them. "Ho, Cousin! Miranda! Happy Beltane. What are you doing here in the woods?"

They stopped and stared. Andrew's lip curled in disgust. "You're unfit to be seen in public, Julian. Go home to bed."

"I am in my cups a bit, but I can't go home. Miranda has been waiting for me, haven't you, love?" He tramped toward them and stumbled on a root, nearly falling. When he reached Miranda, he slapped an arm around her shoulder. "I'll walk you home."

She shrugged free of him, wrinkling her nose. "In the state you're in, I daresay you need someone to walk *you* home."

"Are you offering to come home with me?"

"Julian, please." Andrew gave him a stern look. "Remember that you're speaking to a lady."

"I'm well aware that Miranda is female." He hooked his arm through hers, grinning at her. "Let's have a walk in the woods to 'fetch in the May,' if you take my meaning."

"Julian!" Andrew warned.

Miranda escaped the drunk's grasp and stepped around to the other side of Andrew. To Julian, she said, "Andrew's been kind enough offer me his escort tonight, and I'm pleased to have his protection."

Julian swayed as he gazed at her. "Leave him here and come into the woods with me."

She shook her head.

Andrew lifted his chin. "She's going nowhere without me tonight."

Julian frowned. "Is that right, Miranda?"

"Quite right."

He tottered for another few seconds and lifted the bottle to his lips. Finding it empty, he tossed it on the ground. He looked back at her and broke into a lop-sided grin. "Very well, then. What an insatiable wench you are. A threesome with my cousin isn't what I had in mind, but if you must have two men, then so be it."

Extending his arms, he lurched forward. He tripped again and grappled for her. In a commotion of ripping fabric and snapping branches, he hit the ground.

"Dear me." He hauled himself to his feet and swept his hair out of his eyes.

Andrew punched him in the face.

Julian stumbled backward, holding his jaw. He bumped into a tree and propped himself against it. "What the hell did you do that for?"

Andrew just stared at him, furious.

His cousin's eyes rolled back in his head, and he slumped to the ground and stopped moving. After a moment, he let out a loud snore.

A soft sob drew Andrew's attention to Miranda. She hung her head and used one hand to hold up the side of her gown. A rip ran from her shoulder to her breast line.

He rushed to her and gathered her in his arms. She put her free arm around his waist and buried her face on his chest, sniffling. He wondered whether her tears were due more to fear or to heart-break. As long as he'd known her, she'd never had eyes for anyone but his cousin. Andrew assumed she was in love with him, a thought that made him slightly nauseous. He hoped after tonight she would give up hope of marrying Julian, but her love for him might not be as easy to forget.

"You're safe now." He kissed the top of her head. "You're safe with me."

"I know." Her voice was muffled, but she stopped sniffling. "I feel more a fool than anything else."

He clenched his jaw. "Nonsense. My cousin is the fool."

CHAPTER THREE

Miranda held on to Andrew, hiding her face from him. For years, she'd been aware that Julian didn't hold his drink well, but in the past she'd caught only glimpses of him in such a state. Then he'd slipped out of whatever ball or rout they were attending to run off to who knew where. Those peeks should have been enough to warn her that he wasn't a gentleman, but she'd never let herself acknowledge the fact.

What a fool she must have seemed to Andrew all these years.

She took a deep breath. Sliding her free arm away from him, she wiped her eyes and forced herself to meet his gaze. "Again tonight, I'm indebted to you."

He looked down at his feet. "On the contrary, I must apologize for my cousin's behavior."

She pressed her palms to her cheeks, trying to cool the heat of her skin. She must have looked a wreck. Thank heaven for the darkness. "I could use a moment to collect myself. Do you mind if we sit?"

"Not at all. I believe there's a large flat rock around the bend."

He led her some twenty feet up the path, his hand resting on the small of her back. The secluded location offered the added advantage of getting Julian out of her sight.

For a few minutes, she and Andrew sat beside each other without speaking. Then a soft feminine giggle carried on the breeze from somewhere deeper in the woods. The muffled sounds of a man's murmuring followed.

She and Andrew looked at one another.

The unseen woman moaned.

Understanding dawned on Miranda. Another couple was trysting not far beyond. Heat rose on the nape of her neck, and her eyes widened as she stared at Andrew.

He gave her a half-suppressed grin. "You see now why I warned you that May Eve celebrations are not fit for ladies."

A low masculine groan drifted out from the woods. *That* was what a man sounded like in the throes of passion. She drew in a ragged breath. Here she was, alone with Andrew Owen in the middle of the night listening to a couple make love. Did he feel any of the wonder she did, or was it only her inexperience that made the moment seem intense?

She looked into her lap. "Clearly you were right."

"I'm sorry I made light of our circumstances." The smile left his voice. "This must be very uncomfortable for you."

"Actually, I can't help feeling rather . . . fascinated."

She felt—or sensed—his body tense. He clenched his hand on his knee. Her words had been too brazen. The new freedom she enjoyed tonight had carried her away.

A louder feminine moan sounded from the woods.

Andrew cleared his throat. "Well, provided that I can get you home safely, I'm sure the experience will do no harm to your character. I've always felt that most ladies are a little too sheltered for their own good. Perhaps this will prevent your being anxious on your wedding night."

For the first time in her life, she imagined a wedding night with someone other than Julian—with *Andrew*. A tingle shivered down her spine. Kissing him had been wonderful. Making love to him . . . she drew in her breath, awed by the thought. It was far too soon to speculate that they might marry, but, gracious, the notion beguiled her.

Somehow, she dared to meet his gaze. "I think it might."

"Ohhh," the man in the woods groaned, growing louder now. "Ohhhhhh!"

Andrew's focus dropped to her mouth. Heat emanated from the nape of her neck again. Just as she wished for him to kiss her, he bent to meet her lips.

This time she anticipated the faint taste of mead and that spicy scent of his, but he was even more intoxicating than she remembered. She kissed him back with hunger and slid her arms around him, amazed by how large and warm he felt.

Her behavior wasn't ladylike, but she couldn't help herself. The kiss they'd shared earlier had been lovely, but now she ached with longing. In the same way that he'd always intimidated her more than anyone else, his touch now gratified her more than anything she'd ever felt before.

All it once, it occurred to her that perhaps he meant more to her than she'd ever admitted to herself. Was it possible she'd been a little bit in love with him for years?

The thought made her gasp. She could scarcely believe she was sharing such intimacy with a man with whom she normally had trouble conversing.

She held him tighter, and he deepened the kiss, sampling her lips with his tongue. She parted them and tasted him.

The next moan reverberating on the breeze came from her own throat. Embarrassed, she broke the kiss and turned her head away from him. Her breathing came quickly. She tried to keep her chest from heaving with obvious lust. Andrew was simply indulging her with a little Beltane play, but her own emotions were running wild. Her body actually trembled with need for him.

She clapped her hand over her mouth. Through her fingers, she said, "Perhaps that's enough experience in one night for a lady who wishes to remain one."

"Of course." He rose and turned his back to her, lifting one hand to his forehead. "Forgive me. I allowed myself to get carried away."

She rather thought *she* was the one at fault, but was too mortified to say so.

"I'll take you home," he said. "Give me a moment to collect myself."

She sat and tried to do the same. Her thoughts were a raging storm. Andrew captivated her. Unlike his cousin, he was a gentleman. His kisses drove her wild. His music lifted her to ecstasy. And it turned out he did respect her playing. Of course, they were meant to be together. Why had she never seen it before?

Did *he* see it?

She looked over at him. He still had his back to her, his hands on his hips as he stared toward the bonfire hill.

As she watched, he turned around to face her. "I'm not sure what to do about Julian. Naturally, I'm tempted to leave him, but if we do, he'll be defense-less to cutthroats."

"I suppose you're right." She stood and glanced toward the area where Julian lay, but she still couldn't see him. As much as he'd disgusted her, she wouldn't want to leave him in harm's way. "Do you think the two of us can drag him home?"

"He's too heavy." He looked back toward the hill. "Maybe some of the villagers will help if I offer them a coin or two. I think I see a few men near the bottom of the hill now."

She followed his line of focus and made out several silhouettes moving in the moonlight. "Yes, and one of them has a tall, funny hat like the flower vendor's beau was wearing. If it's him, I'd wager he'll help."

"Right. I'll be back in a moment. Don't worry—I won't leave your sight." He dashed off toward the men.

Miranda stood and watched him, still throbbing with longing. She heard a snore come from Julian and realized that otherwise the woods had gone quiet. When had the other couple finished their lovemaking? She'd been too absorbed with Andrew to notice.

In the distance, he drew near the villagers. She strained her eyes and saw the man with the hat clap him on the back in a friendly manner. With any luck, they would help.

She walked to the spot where Julian lay. He hadn't even changed positions. His hair was splayed over his face, and a small cut on his lip had dried blood caked around it. She felt a tug of pity that he should be seen by the villagers in such a dis-graceful state. Kneeling, she pushed his hair out of his face.

"Miranda Jane!" a voice boomed behind her.

She started but instantly recognized her father's voice. Pressing a hand to her heart, she looked around. "Papa."

He lunged forward and grabbed her under the arms, hefting her away and to her feet. "I never thought I'd find *my* daughter trysting in the woods on May Eve."

"I'm not trysting." *Not now,* she thought, a twinge of guilt mixing in with her fear. His physical handling unnerved her. Her father hadn't touched her at all since she was a child.

"Miranda, I *have* two eyes." He brushed past her and stared down at Julian, who had begun to stir. "At least you're with Ellsworth. He'll make an honest woman of you. It's time he came up to scratch, anyway."

"No, Papa! I'm not with Julian." Panic gripped her. She couldn't marry Julian now. She looked up the hill. Andrew and the others had started moving but were progressing slowly. She didn't know whether or not to tell her father she'd really been with Andrew. Would Papa then press *him* to marry her? If she married, she wanted the decision to be hers and her groom's. "I came to the bonfire on my own."

"Next you'll tell me that you tore your frock on a branch." He leaned over and hauled Julian into a standing position, holding him up by the collar. "To your feet, Ellsworth. What have you to say for yourself?"

Julian squinted and frowned. His eyes crossed and finally fixed on the older man. "Sir Wilfred?"

"You stink of alcohol." He pulled tighter on the younger man's collar. "Tell me, did you rip my daughter's dress? I warn you, don't lie to me."

Julian lifted an eyebrow. He looked toward Miranda and frowned again. His gaze dropped to the tear in her neckline. "Ah, I remember. It was an accident. I fell and must have caught onto her dress. I'll pay for the damage."

"You'll pay all right." Her father let go of him and gave him a shove.

"No, Father!" Miranda shouted.

He turned his back to her. Still staring at Julian, he crossed his arms over his chest. "You'll be marrying her now, you know."

Julian staggered backward and fell against a tree. He focused on Miranda and let his gaze slither down her body until she felt sick. Looking back to Sir Wilfred, he swallowed. "That's always been the plan. Nothing has changed."

"Yes, it has. Tomorrow I'll inform your father of your transgressions, and we'll have the vicar start reading the banns this Sunday. You two will be married in June." Spinning around to Miranda, he grabbed her under one arm and tugged her toward the path. "Come on. Let's get you out of here before that group of ruffians approaching sees you."

"But Andrew—Mr. Owen—is with those men." She tried to look back toward him, but her father dragged her into the woods. "He'll tell you what happened. He's been with me all evening—and *he's* not in his cups. He's a gentleman."

"Andrew Owen may try to cover for his cousin, but that doesn't change your predicament. Even if he was with you two, he's no chaperon. You've been disgraced and you must marry to save your reputation and that of your family. 'Tis about time, too. You ought to be happy."

"But I don't want to marry Julian. I came to realize that tonight, Papa."

He snorted. "Then you realized it too late. You

should have done so before you stole out with him and let him ruin you."

"I'm not ruined." Her throat closed up and choked off her voice. As her father towed her, stumbling, along the path, she wondered how she could possibly tell him she wanted Andrew, when she didn't know if Andrew wanted her. Andrew had indulged her tonight for the sake of May Eve, but they hadn't even discussed tomorrow. For all she knew, he was leaving Gladstone on the morn and wouldn't be back for a year.

"You *are* ruined, Miranda," her father said. "Those villagers may well have seen you with Ellsworth. If not, someone must have seen you earlier."

"Papa," she croaked out, "please speak to Mr. Owen. Please, let's go back and talk to him."

He stopped and turned to look at her. "What does he have to do with anything?"

She dropped her gaze. His tight grip on her arm humiliated her, made her feel powerless. "He and I spent some time together tonight. We . . . we both share a love of music . . ."

Her father shook his head. "You are *not* going to turn fickle on me, Miranda. I don't know what has gotten into you, first stealing out and now entertaining thoughts of men other than your intended. You're lucky I don't beat you after this disgrace."

He pulled her forward again, and she struggled to match his pace without tripping. A sob slipped out of her. She'd never seen him so angry and didn't know if indeed he might hit her.

Frightened, she bit her lip to try to hold back her tears. His firmness gave her little hope that he might change his mind about insisting that she marry Julian. Perhaps she could convince her mother to intervene with him enough to delay the reading of the banns. That would give her time to visit Andrew and try to gauge his feelings for her.

Not that she could really expect him to rescue her. Before tonight, he'd probably never thought twice about her. He certainly wasn't likely to be prepared to marry her in his cousin's stead. Was even he thinking of her now, or had he forgotten their kisses already?

Who knew what men thought of such things?

"Who's that?" the flower vendor's lover asked, looking off to the bottom of the hill.

Andrew followed his gaze and saw a burly figure with Miranda and his cousin, gesticulating wildly. *Sir Wilfred,* he realized. His stomach clenched in fear for her. Only fragments of the man's words carried up the hill, but his exaggerated movements showed he was angry. "It's her father."

"Cor!" one of the other men said.

The others stopped in their tracks. One said, "We don't want hide nor hair of that."

Andrew started running down the hill.

"Good luck, mate!" one of the villagers called after him.

Andrew ignored him. The scene at the bottom of the hill demanded all his attention. As he sidestepped a boulder, he saw Sir Wilfred grab Miranda and haul her by one arm toward the path.

"Wait!" he yelled—but they disappeared into the woods, either not hearing or disregarding him.

Perhaps it wasn't wise to hail them anyway. What could he say to Sir Wilfred? If he told him that Miranda had been with him all night, he'd be lucky if the man didn't kill him before he got a chance to mention his good intentions. Better to call at

Granville Lodge in the morning, which was only a few hours away. He would tell Sir Wilfred that he wanted to court Miranda. His chances of acceptance would be better if the man didn't know he was involved with her excursion tonight.

He slowed and noticed his cousin leaning against a tree. Jogging up to him, he asked, "What happened?"

"I'm still trying to sort that out. Where did you come from?" Julian rubbed his temples. He met Andrew's gaze, and his brow crinkled. "Weren't you here earlier?"

Andrew frowned. "You don't remember?"

He shook his head, then put his fingers up to feel his lip. "Ow. Hell. Now I remember—you hit me!"

Andrew put his hands on his hips. "You insulted Miranda."

"Did I?" His indignation ebbed as quickly as it had come. He looked skyward, rubbing his jaw. "What did I say?"

"I'm hardly about to repeat it." Andrew looked toward the path in the woods. Turning back to Julian, he asked, "You don't think her father will do her harm, do you?"

"He seemed more apt to injure me. He says that I have to marry her now." He twisted his mouth. Suddenly, he met Andrew's gaze and tilted his head to one side. "Wait a minute, did you and Miranda come to the bonfire together?"

Andrew was still reeling from his cousin's first statement. Sir Wilfred was finally pressing Julian to get to the altar! Surely Miranda wouldn't agree to marry him after tonight . . . would she? He felt sick. When he'd kissed her, she had definitely responded—but that didn't mean she was over her feelings for the man who had always been her intended.

He forced himself to face his cousin. "Her father wants you to marry her?"

Julian narrowed his eyes. "What's it to you?"

"I don't have the impression you want to marry her."

He hesitated and swallowed. "You know I've always planned to do so."

"Have you indeed?" Andrew stepped closer, looking down his nose at him from just inches away. "You told me you've never even kissed her."

Julian scowled and looked off into the trees. "She's not the sort to bestow favors on a man before he's made a declaration."

"Isn't she?" Andrew just stared until his cousin met his gaze again. If a hint of satisfaction crept into his countenance, he didn't care enough to stop it.

Julian steeled his jaw. "I don't know what you've been playing at tonight, Cuz, but Miranda and I have been intended for each other since childhood. You'll do well to remember that. She's never had eyes for anyone but me."

The flash of confidence Andrew felt evaporated. He'd witnessed exactly what his cousin described. Was there any chance that nearly twenty years of devotion could be undone in one night? If Julian pulled himself together and visited Miranda to smooth things over with her, her vexation with him might well melt.

Cold fear shot through him. He turned away, unwilling to look into his rival's face. Starting toward Ellsworth Manor, he said over his shoulder, "I'm going home."

He would have to clean himself up and visit Granville Lodge before he lost his nerve. Sir Wilfred might not even let him see his daughter—and the baronet was less likely than she to set aside plans made two decades ago. Naturally, he would favor Julian over Andrew, thanks to Julian's title and greater wealth. Andrew would have to convince the man that he had something more valuable than worldly possessions to offer Miranda.

"Suit yourself," his cousin called after him, "but the night isn't over yet. Personally, I think I'll have another go at Betsy the barmaid."

Andrew stopped, tempted to go back and land his cousin another facer. Then he decided to let Julian drown in his debauchery. Another visit to Betsy would keep his cousin from getting to Granville Lodge before he did.

"Very well," he said, and started walking again, this time with more vigor. He didn't look back.

When he reached the manor, the first rays of morning sunlight had just started lightening the sky. He dismayed the sleepy servants by ordering an immediate bath. After washing, he dressed in his finest coat and breeches and rode to Granville Lodge.

Though he arrived too early for a polite visit, Sir Wilfred received him. In fact, when Andrew walked into his den, the man didn't appear surprised—nor did he rise to shake hands.

"Good morning, Sir," Andrew said. "Thank you for seeing me."

From behind his desk, the baronet gave him a dispassionate look. "Mr. Owen, you might as well save your breath. You and I have nothing to discuss."

Andrew froze. How much did he know? His cold reception didn't bode well, but did the man really understand his purpose in coming? He cleared his throat. "I beg to differ, sir. We . . . we need to discuss your daughter's future."

The baronet took out a pouch of tobacco and began filling his pipe. "Miranda's future is settled. Perhaps your cousin Ellsworth hasn't yet told you, but he and she will be married next month."

"Julian did tell me, several hours ago, that you . . . urged him to marry your daughter soon. Sir, you saw his state this morning. You must have noticed that he's rather . . . susceptible to drink. Frankly, he isn't the most responsible man, and I'm convinced your daughter wouldn't be happy with him. Dare I say it, I want to court her myself."

The baronet lit his pipe. "Ellsworth has a title and a horde of money. He can support Miranda in far better style than you can."

"But will he give her the respect—and love—she deserves? Though my prospects can't match his, I assure you they're acceptable—as is my conduct, unlike his."

The older man exhaled swirls of smoke, watching them rise. "She won't have you, Owen. She's been meant for your cousin nearly all her life, and she has always welcomed the arrangement. The objections you raise are immaterial. 'Tis normal for a young man to sow some oats."

"Let me talk to her."

"She doesn't want to see you." Sir Wilfred met his gaze. "I believe there was some ill-conceived dalliance between you two last night, but Miranda knows where her duty lies."

Andrew's stomach coiled. It was exactly as he'd feared. One evening hadn't been enough to convince her they were meant to be together. "Please, let me speak to her just this once."

"I'm afraid I'm going to have to ask you to leave, Mr. Owen." He reached for the bell pull and tugged. "Take a lesson from Miranda and think about your own duties. This betrayal of your cousin doesn't become you."

The butler appeared in the doorway. "Yes, Sir Wilfred?"

"Mr. Owen is leaving," the baronet said.

Andrew stared at him, unsure whether he should be angry or ashamed. Likely the latter. He'd known for years that Miranda was out of his reach. How had he dared believe that a few hours with her could change a lifetime of resolution?

He couldn't speak, so he nodded to the baronet and left.

CHAPTER FOUR

After May Eve, Miranda's father confined her to her bedchamber. The only visitors he permitted were her mother and the housekeeper, and even them he supervised. His stony stare made her dread speaking in front of him, but every time he and the others came she forced herself to ask if anyone had called for her. She prayed that Andrew would try to see her, but according to them, only Lady Elizabeth had stopped by—not even Julian.

After three days, she worked up the courage to ask to be allowed out of her chamber. Her father ignored the request and, as usual, locked the door on his way out.

That night she contemplated sneaking out. As mad as repeating her folly would be, she was desperate to see Andrew, even if it meant throwing pebbles at his chamber window at Ellsworth. She got to the point of rising and dressing after midnight, but when she looked outside, she found a footman posted on the balcony.

More than a week went by, and finally her mother entered the room alone one day.

Miranda set aside the book she'd been reading and sat up in bed. Without her father present, she hoped her mother might show her some mercy.

"When will I be allowed out of this room, Mother? The lack of exercise can't be healthy. Isn't there some way you can appeal to Father for me?"

A mix of emotions flickered across her mother's face. She looked downward. "Your father says you may come out for your betrothal party. That's why I'm here to see you. We've made arrangements to hold the gathering here in two weeks' time."

Miranda swallowed. If she was ever going to speak, now was the time. "Mama, do you realize I don't want to marry Julian?"

A long pause ensued. Her mother kneaded her hands in her lap. "The match was made long ago, Miranda. Perhaps there was a time when we had the leeway to change our plans, but you sealed your fate when you stole out to meet Julian on May Eve."

"But you don't know everything that happened that night. Julian behaved dreadfully." She got out of bed, paced a few steps away, and then turned back around to face her. "You must have noticed how he drinks at parties. This was the worst I've ever seen him. Andrew Owen had to protect me from his advances. Did Papa tell you that?"

"I knew only that both cousins were present." She met her daughter's gaze. "Julian ripped your gown?"

"Yes."

She frowned. "If his cousin hadn't been there, do you think he would have taken liberties with you against your will?"

"He might have tried." She drew in a shaky breath. "I don't know—but I know I want to be with Andrew, not Julian. Unfortunately, I can't say for certain that Andrew returns my feelings."

Her mother rose and went to the window, staring out. "I'm afraid that Mr. Owen is gone, love. He left

Gladstone on May Day. Lady Ellsworth mentioned it while she and I were planning your party."

Miranda's jaw went slack. Tears filled her eyes. He didn't love her, then—or perhaps he was too loyal to his family to betray Julian. But she was convinced Julian didn't care about her. Couldn't Andrew see that?

Her mother turned around and gave her a look that was almost a wince. "Please, Miranda, be reasonable. You've been aware of our plans for you since childhood. Until now, you've never voiced a word of doubt. You must recapture what you felt for Julian for all of those years. I daresay he'll mature with marriage."

A tear rolled down Miranda's cheek. She didn't trust herself to speak. If she did, something rebellious was bound to come out. Lord help her, but she *wouldn't* marry Julian. Her feelings for him would never return to what they'd been. May Eve was only the culmination of years of gradual disillusion. Now that she'd finally realized she didn't love him, she knew she never would.

"Think about it, dear." Her gaze averted, her mother bent and kissed her on the forehead, then left the room.

Miranda let out a sob. She flopped down on the bed and buried her face in a pillow. More than anything, she wished that she could see Andrew and at least try to glean how much he felt for her. Was there any chance he would be at the betrothal party?

Not unless he attends because he wants to give Julian and me his blessing, she thought. Unfortunately, if Andrew cared for her but didn't want to betray his cousin, he would avoid the party. Surely if he were inclined to challenge the betrothal, he'd be at Granville Lodge now, beating down the door.

Her case seemed hopeless—but there was one vow to herself that she refused to compromise. She had never wanted a loveless marriage, and she wouldn't settle for one now.

She flipped over on her back and stared at the ceiling. If she couldn't talk her parents out of this wedding, she would simply have to flee. She didn't know where she'd go, but she wouldn't marry against her will. If worse came to worse, she would lie to a distant relative or an old governess in order to stay with them to buy time.

Of course, escaping wouldn't be easy with her father posting sentries around the house. She took a deep breath. Perhaps if she pretended to submit to his wishes, he would begin to let down his guard.

She would keep watch for the right moment, and when it came, she'd be gone.

Her decision made, she dedicated the next two weeks to softening her parents' will. First she told them that she had thought long and hard about her last conversation with her mother and, though difficult, she would *try* to recapture the feelings she'd had for Julian before May Eve. Her mother sighed aloud, and her father conceded that it was a step in the right direction.

For each of the following few days, she brought up one good point related to marrying Julian, trying hard to make her capitulation appear feasible.

"I have to admit," she said to her father the first day, "I do like the idea of continuing to live here in Gladstone. Being close to my family will always be a comfort."

A day later she mused to her mother, "You know, I

have always looked forward to having Elizabeth for a sister. I couldn't ask for a closer friend."

The next time they both visited her, she said, "Ellsworth Manor has such an excellent pianoforte. I must say I shall enjoy playing *that* instrument every day."

When her mother suggested bringing in a seamstress to start work on the wedding dress, Miranda hesitated, nodded, and forced a small smile. The woman grinned broadly in return. The fitting sessions were so close to enjoyable that it saddened Miranda. If her parents had acted reasonably, perhaps she might have been planning her wedding in truth.

By the week of the party, there was still a guard posted outside her window, but her parents allowed her to eat her meals downstairs and to play pianoforte for an hour a day. Her mother invited her on occasional walks around the grounds, though two footmen always escorted them. Perhaps it was best that the servants were present to keep Miranda from confiding her true feelings again, anyway. She kept quiet, her head so full of Andrew that she had little patience for making light conversation.

In bed on the night before the gathering, she wondered if the following evening her parents might allow her a private walk in the garden with Julian. Was that too much for a betrothed couple to ask? If they insisted on having footmen watch her, perhaps she could persuade Julian to bribe the servants for a few minutes alone.

In fact, Julian might well be drinking. She opened her eyes and stared into the darkness. For once, she rather hoped he wouldn't be in top form. If he drank, he'd be easier to fool—and to slip away from.

She rolled over onto her side, too nervous to sleep. The wedding was only two weeks away now. Likely, the party offered her best chance for escape. If only Julian passed out in the garden, she might have time to grab her horse and fly.

It was a long shot. She'd be lucky if she got a minute to run into the woods.

A better idea occurred to her: Instead of wandering into the garden with him, she'd ask him to meet her in a secluded room of the house. He wouldn't immediately realize she wasn't going to show up, and by the time he alerted the others that she was missing, she'd be farther away.

She could flee to the home of her Great Aunt Letty, who lived in Penrith—not far from Andrew. The poor old lady could likely be persuaded that they'd arranged the visit the last time they spoke. At this point, almost nothing seemed too shameful. She would try to see Andrew before anyone caught up with her. Frankly, she hoped he'd elope with her. Perhaps her isolation was driving her to madness, but she'd nearly convinced herself there had been a spark between the two of them for years.

Now if only she could convince him.

During the time that Miranda's wild plans were germinating, Andrew sat home in despair. Though he didn't receive an invitation to the betrothal party, his mother mentioned hers, so he knew Miranda was going ahead with the wedding. After coming so close to winning her, he couldn't accept losing her. The memory of the passion he'd felt between them during that last kiss haunted him. She had wanted him for those moments; he was certain of it. Did she ever think of him now?

He tried to muster his pride—and his family loyalty—enough to avoid begging her to see him, but he knew she'd be happier with him than she would with his cousin. Her father had said she knew where her duty lay—with her family, presumably. Well, what about what was due to her? She deserved better treatment than Julian dealt her!

After the first week, he broke down and wrote to her. Whether the letter would make it past her father and reach her, he didn't know.

Once he'd posted it, his dissatisfaction lingered. The temptation to return to Gladstone and force an audience with her plagued him. In his imagination, he visualized scenes in which he burst into her bedchamber and seduced her. Other times, he imagined bursting in and facing her horrified screams.

One afternoon nearly three weeks into this hell, the post arrived. As usual, he hurried to check for a response from her.

With a sinking heart, he saw that none had come.

He did have a letter from Monsieur Desroches, though. The chance that the maestro would have something to say about Miranda stirred his interest.

He opened the parchment and read the following:

Dear Mr. Owen,

My obligations in Penrith have come to a close, and I am now free to call on your talented Miss Granville. Once again, I appreciate your referring her to me, as well as your offer of escort to Gladstone. Please meet at the White Hart Inn on the morning of June first, and we shall travel the remainder of the journey together. I look forward to seeing both you and your protégée.

Yours, etc.
David Desroches

Andrew grimaced. He'd forgotten his promise to the maestro. His chagrin, however, wasn't because he anticipated disappointing the man. He had no intention of reneging. On the contrary, he would go to Gladstone with Monsieur Desroches and, somehow, he would see Miranda. The part he didn't like was the risk of making a complete fool of himself.

He scribbled a note to Sir Wilfred informing him that Monsieur Desroches would be calling on his daughter. He neglected to mention that he, too, would be in town.

On June first, he met the maestro at the White Hart and they climbed into Andrew's carriage. The ride to Gladstone took a good twelve hours. By the time they'd made it to the village inn, Andrew had told his teacher much of the dilemma he faced.

Being French, Desroches was rather romantic.

"Well, we shall abduct her zees evening, of course," he said, with a deadpan expression. "It ees your only recourse. I will help you."

Andrew thought the plan a bit excessive, but he did want to try to see her. Unsure whether he intended to plead with her father or sneak into Miranda's chamber, he left Monsieur at the inn and drove toward Granville Lodge.

When he turned into the drive, he found several carriages waiting ahead of him outside the front entrance. Black-clad men and bejeweled women alighted and entered the house. Obviously a large party was in progress, not the best time to approach Sir Wilfred—or was it? In front of his guests, the man wouldn't want to make a scene.

His luggage was still in the carriage. He rummaged through a portmanteau, found a black jacket and shrugged into it.

Climbing out of the gig, he handed his reins to

a footman. A queue of guests waited at the door to be received. Observing that the servants were all too busy to notice him, he slipped around the side of the house, thinking to enter through a secondary door.

As he'd hoped, enough guests hovered on the terrace for him to blend in easily. Several acquaintances greeted him as if he belonged there. Apparently, Sir Wilfred hadn't made it known that he wasn't welcome. The man had likely kept quiet about May Eve, not wanting to spread the story about his daughter.

A passing servant offered him a glass of champagne, and he accepted, trying to look nonchalant as he sipped. Inside, his guts twisted into a knot. Would he manage to speak to Miranda? If so, would this be the last time ever?

"To the happy couple," an old schoolmate of his said to him, raising a glass. "I never thought I'd see the day when your cousin settled down."

Andrew made a futile attempt to smile. Damned if he would drink to *that*.

Luckily the man was distracted by an attractive local widow, who pulled him aside to speak in private.

Evidently Andrew had walked in on the betrothal party. He should have realized as much. He took a swig of champagne and attempted to gather enough courage to enter the house.

A pianoforte inside struck the first few notes of Bach's *Piano Concerto Number Five*.

He froze. That was the composition Miranda had mentioned as a favorite on May Eve. As the pianist plunged into the melody, he recognized the technique for hers.

Wandering to a pair of open French doors, he

looked inside and saw her at the keyboard. His pulse quickened. Her eyes were closed and her delicate brows turned up in an expression of intense emotion.

She said she plays this song when she wants to escape her life, he remembered.

As the song broke into a cascade of quick notes, she opened her eyes and sensed his stare. Her gaze met his, and she missed a note. She sucked in her breath, then continued playing, her eyes still fixed on him.

He let his gaze burn into hers, trying to send her a message. *I love you,* he thought, his teeth clenched.

Her chest swelled, and she struck the chords harder, never looking away from him. He had no doubt she wanted to tell him something, too.

Swallowing his misgivings, he entered the house. He wove through the crowded room, none of the faces but hers registering with him. Half expecting her father or Julian to grab him by the collar any minute and throw him out, he went to the pianoforte and sat down beside her, saying nothing.

She reached the end of the sheet of music before her. He turned the page for her, his fingers trembling.

"I'm not going to marry Julian," she said quietly.

Joy washed through him. Through a tight throat, he managed to croak, "Good."

She glanced around the room, then looked back to the sheet music, playing on. "Unfortunately, my father is determined that I go through with the wedding. He has locked me in my bedchamber for weeks."

Reality flooded back. He drew in a deep breath and scanned the room. Neither Sir Wilfred nor Julian was in the immediate vicinity. Many guests were watching Miranda, but they all wore faint smiles. None looked disturbed by his presence. "Did you receive my letter?"

Executing a beautiful crescendo, she said, "No, I haven't received any communications since May Eve."

He frowned. "I wasn't invited here, so we must speak quickly, before your parents cast me out. What can I do to help you?"

"I have a plan to escape tonight. Do you have your carriage with you?"

"Yes."

"Leave now and drive to the hill where the villagers held the bonfire on May Eve. Within a quarter hour, I'll steal out of here. Meet me by the hill, where the path that we took that night emerges."

"I will." He turned the page for her again and rose. Bowing, he said under his breath, "Be careful."

"You, too."

He strode back toward the door he'd entered, scanning the room again and finding no sign of his adversaries. At the threshold, he looked back at Miranda one last time.

She met his gaze as she played out the final notes of the composition. The guests broke into polite applause. An admirer approached her, and she finally looked away, rising to accept his compliments.

It was Julian, Andrew realized. When had his cousin entered in the room? Had Julian seen him?

He ducked out the door and walked briskly toward the stables, glancing back over his shoulder. No one appeared to take note of his exit.

At the stables, he told the groom that he'd received a message about a personal emergency. The lad retrieved his horses and carriage, and Andrew left without delay.

He led the pair of grays in a brisk trot up the drive, periodically glancing back over his shoulder. There was still no one behind him. Would Miranda be able to get away? He wished he'd asked how she planned to elude her father and Julian, but there hadn't been time. Had either of them seen him speaking to her? Would an acquaintance mention seeing him?

A carriage approached from the other direction. The coachman tipped his hat to Andrew as he passed. Not recognizing the livery, he nodded. He hoped the occupants hadn't recognized him, either.

He turned onto the road and urged the horses into a gallop, though hurrying was pointless. He was sure to have to wait for Miranda. The path through the woods was shorter than the route by road, but on foot she would be longer.

Still no one following, he thought, looking back once again. He prayed that Miranda had the same luck. The idea of her running through the woods alone worried him nearly as much as that of her being detained at home. He decided that when he reached the hill, he would tie the horses and hit the path on foot to meet her.

The ride seemed interminable, but he finally reached the hill and stowed the gig behind a high hedge. He tied the horses to an oak tree and headed on foot to the meeting place Miranda had specified.

Returning to that spot was strange. The weather was similar to what it had been on May Eve—crisp and clear—but while on that night shouts and music had echoed through the woods, tonight only crickets made their presence known.

He reached the top of the path and paused to glance back at the horses. The moon shone bright, and he could just make out their silhouettes. Both bent over to graze, obviously content on their own.

Hoping they'd be safe, he started up the path. As much as he would hate to lose them to thieves, Miranda's well-being was a bigger concern.

He had only gone twenty or thirty yards when he thought he heard a noise ahead in the woods. Stopping to listen, he distinguished the sounds of splintering branches and crunching underbrush. Someone—or something—was approaching fast. Surely Miranda would move with more grace. It was likely a buck or a large badger.

Or an avenger after me, he thought.

Climbing onto a boulder, he grabbed a thick branch and hoisted himself into a tree. The leaves would camouflage him from an irate Sir Wilfred or Julian, but they also prevented him from seeing out.

As the noises neared, he distinguished a pattern of alternating crunching. The interloper was on two feet—a man.

His shoulders sagged. Where was Miranda, then? He doubted she'd even made it out of Granville Lodge. Likely, the footmen had discovered her, and her father and Julian had roughed her up until she confessed her plan.

He surmised that it was Julian approaching now— certainly if their roles had been reversed, Andrew wouldn't have let his cousin get away with trying to abduct his fiancée. If Julian didn't spot him in the tree, he would definitely find the gig out by the hill. Andrew's only hope was to catch him by surprise.

Grabbing onto a higher branch, he pulled his feet up beneath him. He poised on his haunches, ready to pounce on whomever passed below.

CHAPTER FIVE

Miranda saw Julian enter the room and jumped up from the bench to greet him. She glanced toward the door where Andrew had been standing, but he'd disappeared.

Thank heaven. They'd been lucky that neither her father nor his cousin had seen him with her. Her mother had actually been in the room during the brief encounter, but Miranda wasn't sure if she'd observed them or not. The baroness had either been too rapt in conversation to notice, or she'd taken pity and chosen to allow them a few minutes together.

"You play like an angel," Julian said, the smell of cognac wafting on his breath. Though he'd arrived at the party no more than a half hour earlier, he'd obviously had a head start on imbibing alcohol. He tilted his head to one side and gave her a crooked grin.

She forced a smile. "Except I play pianoforte rather than the harp."

"Well, you *look* like an angel, then." He leaned against the wall, and his gaze slid to her cleavage.

Her lip curled in disdain, even though she'd chosen a low-cut neckline hoping to lure him into a rendezvous. Fortunately he wasn't focused on her mouth. She cleared her throat and schooled her features into blandness. "Julian, I'd, er, like some time alone with you tonight."

"Would you?" His gaze shot back to meet hers. "Shall we take a turn in the garden?"

She moistened her lips. "Actually, I fear my father may have footmen posted on the terrace ready to follow me through the gardens." As if on cue, out of the corner of her eye, she saw the baronet enter from the card room. She leaned close to Julian and nearly cracked her face trying to smile. "I was hoping for . . . a bit more seclusion."

He raised his eyebrows, then grinned. "Indeed?"

She glanced back at her father and found that he was watching them with a look of satisfaction. He nodded to her and turned back into the card room. She felt sick at having to deceive him, but to obey him would be worse. To Julian, she said, "Do you know where the morning room is located?"

"Yes, in the very rear of the Lodge—an excellent location for a tryst, I daresay." He laughed.

"Hush, or someone will overhear. Make your way there as soon as possible, and I'll meet you shortly— say, in about a quarter hour."

"Excellent. I'll grab a drink and head back there now." He moved toward a servant carrying a tray of champagne saucers. Taking one, he glanced back at her and winked. Then he headed toward the rear of the house.

She turned in the opposite direction, toward the ladies' retiring room. Brushing past guests, she smiled, nodded, and repeatedly murmured an excuse about her hem coming down. At the door to the ladies' room, she stood back to allow two of Julian's elderly aunts to exit. For an instant no one was watching, so she ducked into a seldom-used sitting room *beside* the ladies' chamber.

Snatching up a modestly sized bag she'd packed and hidden behind the drapes that afternoon, she poked her head out an open window. The moon shone bright—a disadvantage for her—but this side of the lawn was peppered with pine trees that cast deep shadows. With that in mind, she'd worn a dark green gown, countering her mother's protests that she ought to wear white with a fabrication that Julian preferred her in sage.

She looked up and down the side of the house. No sign of movement. This side of the Lodge had no terrace, so guests weren't likely to be wandering here. Climbing over the window sill, she made the short drop to the ground and ran like the wind. Her skirt hampered her somewhat, but the soft slippers she'd worn served her well.

At the nearest stand of pines, she glanced back. No one followed, so she dashed for the next group of trees. The most important thing was to get to the bonfire hill as quickly as possible.

Luckily, she knew the grounds like the back of her hand. A short bridle path cut through to the road, emerging conveniently close to the footpath that would lead her to Andrew. She sprinted for the length of the bridle path, leaping over ruts and soiling her slippers in dried horse manure.

When she reached the footpath through the woods, her throat stung from breathing hard, and a stitch cut into her side. She couldn't run any farther, but she dragged herself with as much speed as she could gather.

As far as she could see, no one was behind her, but she never dared to stop and listen.

The question remained whether Andrew would be at the end of the path. She thought chances were good that he had escaped the party without trouble.

He'd left via the terrace and would have cut through the garden to the stables. With any luck, he would beat her to the hill.

And where will we go from there? she wondered, holding her ribcage as she struggled onward. He'd offered to help her, but marrying her was quite a different matter. If he did ask, she prayed it wasn't because he felt obliged—yet how would she know for certain?

She slowed to a trudge, her heart pounding. Perspiration broke on her brow, and a droplet rolled down one temple. An owl gave an eerie hoot above her, reminding her that she was alone in the woods. Gooseflesh rose on her bare forearms. At every bend in the path, she worried that around it a wild animal or a cutthroat might await her.

At last, the bonfire hill, outlined in moonlight, came into view in the distance.

Andrew wasn't in sight.

Her stomach constricted. *Please let him be just around the corner with his carriage and horses,* she thought. She quickened her pace again.

Suddenly, a dark form swept down from a tree in front of her. She yelped, tripped on a root, and fell forward. Fortunately, her bag cushioned the impact.

"Miranda!" a male voice intoned.

Springing to her feet again, she saw that it was Andrew. She clapped her hand over her heart, joy rushing through her body. "Good heavens! You gave me a fright."

"Pray pardon." He stepped forward and studied her face, his own brow furrowed. "Are you injured?"

"No." One of her arms stung as if scraped, but she was too nervous to care. "I'm fine."

"I expected Julian or your father, not you." He kneaded his forehead. "Foolish of me."

"No harm done." She brushed off her skirt and glanced into the darkness behind them. "We need to get out of here. Is your carriage near?"

"Out by the road." He took her bag from her. "Come along."

They walked briskly. When she spotted the carriage, she broke into a run, and he followed suit.

The horses whinnied as they approached.

"Hush," Andrew told them, fumbling to untie the reins in haste.

Miranda gave their noses a quick rub. "Am I glad to see you." She didn't linger, however, climbing into the gig before Andrew was even ready to help her.

He joined her on the box and lifted the reins. "To the main road?"

"Please."

The carriage lurched forward, and she grasped the bench for support. As they pulled out into the lane, she looked forward and behind them. Over the pound of galloping hooves, she shouted, "Still no one in sight."

"Whoa, fellows!" Andrew adjusted the horses to a swift but less violent pace. Turning to Miranda, he asked, "Do you think anyone saw you leave?"

"No, but it won't take long for them to notice I'm gone. The longer we can go without a passerby seeing us, the better."

"How did you get away?"

"I asked Julian to meet me for a tryst in the back of the house. Then I told half a dozen other people I'd torn my gown, went to the room beside the ladies' chamber, and climbed out the window. I'm not sure how long Julian will wait before he starts looking for me."

He snorted. "With any luck, he'll pass out and neglect to sound the alarm at all."

She let out a nervous laugh, venting the tension she'd had bottled up. "I had that thought, too, but, of course, I can't count on it."

Traveling was still fairly noisy, and they rode for several minutes without speaking again. The silence gave her time to absorb the enormity of what she'd done—and what Andrew had done for her. She'd dragged him into this scheme without giving him a chance to consider the consequences, she realized. Unlike her, he hadn't spent the last few weeks planning to throw away all pretense of respectability.

What did he expect to happen tonight? Did he want to elope with her, or was he merely spiriting her away from his cousin?

She swallowed against a tightening in her throat and looked at him. He held his gaze intent on the road, his strong chin high and noble. A pang of love for him pierced her like a blade. All she'd done was ask him, and in an instant he'd staked his reputation for her.

He slowed the horses as they approached the junction of the main thoroughfare. Looking at her, he asked, "Did you plan to head north or south?"

She opened her mouth, but no sound came out. She'd intended to head south and try to see him, but with him here, what she really wanted was to elope to Gretna Green, where they could marry without a license. Unfortunately, he hadn't asked her to marry him. "I . . . er, I'm not certain."

They neared the intersection, and the horses slowed to a trot. The night loomed quiet, and an unspoken question hung in the air. He glanced behind them and then at her, moistening his lips. "To Scotland, perhaps?"

"Yes," she said. Her heart beat wildly. Was he thinking of eloping? "Yes, to Scotland."

He turned the horses northward and stepped up the pace again. Though he fixed his gaze on the road, she suspected he was concentrating on something else—maybe debating whether or not to propose to her. Unless he truly wanted to marry her, she didn't want him to ask.

She cleared her throat and said, "Andrew, I must apologize. I've been planning to flee for weeks, but you had less than a moment to think about the possible ramifications. I shouldn't have asked you to help me."

He shook his head. "I did think about the consequences. I'd much rather be driving you to Scotland now than watching you pretend to celebrate your betrothal to Julian."

"But now you risk facing the anger of my father and the censure of your family." She bit her lip. "Perhaps no one need ever learn that you helped me run away."

"That's not necessarily what I want." He met her gaze, his expression serious. "I'm glad you had the courage to resist marrying against your will . . . but I hope you can find it in your heart to consider marrying me."

She drew in a swift breath. Consider it? She wanted it with all her soul—and body. "But do *you* want to marry me? I won't have a marriage without love."

Taking the reins in one hand, he placed the other one over hers. "Miranda, I've loved you for so long, I can't remember when I first knew it."

Her heart jumped in her chest.

"Oh, I love you, too." Her voice cracked. "I think I've loved you for years, but I never admitted it to myself until May Eve."

He lifted her hand and kissed it. "Then we'll marry the moment we reach Gretna Green."

"Yes." She grinned. "Give me a kiss. Please."

He bent and brushed her lips with his. The bumpy ride made the effort rather haphazard. He laughed. "Dare we stop and have a proper snog?"

They both looked back at the road behind them. In the distance, the faint light of a carriage lantern glowed.

Her stomach clenched. She turned back to Andrew.

His face was grim. "Not yet, it seems."

He took the reins in both hands and looked to the horses, urging them on faster.

She shifted closer to him, reveling in his warmth and that hint of spicy scent that she recognized as his. If she hadn't been so scared that her father would find a way to stop them, she would have been in heaven.

Andrew glanced back over his shoulder, careful not to wake Miranda, who had just slumped against his shoulder in sleep. They'd been driving for hours, and the faint light behind them had finally disappeared about a quarter hour earlier. He had no idea whether the other carriage held other travelers or someone in pursuit of them, but it appeared to have stopped—hopefully for the night.

He didn't dare lose time on the road for sleep, but his horses were exhausted and would never make it to Gretna Green without rest.

With an arm around Miranda to steady her, he urged the pair on. He still could scarcely believe she was here with him and had accepted his proposal. Until they were lawfully married, he wouldn't quite feel secure.

At the first inn they came upon, he woke the

owner and negotiated to hire fresh horses, reluctantly leaving his grays stabled there. He also bought a hamper of bread, cheese, and wine. He and Miranda continued driving, snacking on some of the food, though he skipped the wine due to his fatigue. Miranda had a few sips and dozed beside him again.

She woke with the first rays of dawn. Stretching her arms, she looked at the road behind them. "Have you seen that lantern behind us at all?"

He shook his head, fighting to keep his eyes open.

"You look as though you could use a nap." She reached for the reins. "I can drive. You lie down in the back."

"You know how to drive a gig?"

"I've been driving for years."

He hated to impose upon her, but he simply couldn't stay awake. He handed her the reins. "Thank you. I'll stay on the box with you, however. Wake me if any trouble arises."

"Of course."

Under the circumstances, he doubted he would sleep much, but when he woke again, the sun was strong and high in the sky. He rubbed his eyes and sat up.

Miranda smiled at him and leaned over to give him a peck on the lips.

His blood rushed. They would be married today. He cupped a hand behind her head and kissed her harder.

She giggled and pressed her forehead against his. "This is the second time I've been out all night with you. Now I'm well and truly compromised."

"Not so much as you will be soon," he said.

She sucked in her breath. "*Very* soon."

He kissed her again. The bumpy ride made it difficult to get much more than a taste of her without bumping noses.

Reluctantly, he backed away and glanced around at the landscape. Rolling hills stretched out on either side of the road. "We must be nearing the border."

"Only an hour or two away, I daresay."

The remainder of the journey flew. In the highest spirits, they planned a wedding journey in the Lake District before returning to face the ire of their families. He told her he regretted he wouldn't be able to support her in as high a style as his cousin, but she assured him that if she had him and a pianoforte, she could yearn for nothing more.

Just outside of Gretna Green, a farmer along the road was able to tell them where to find the nearest civil "priest" in town. When they reached the man's house, a modest but attractive cottage, it had only just gone seven o'clock. They had to knock several times before a sleepy-eyed servant answered the door.

Andrew apologized and explained why they'd come.

"Not to worry." The matronly woman yawned but stood back, holding the door for them to enter. "We get 'em at all hours. Had an urgent ceremony last night in the wee hours, so Mr. Rickert is still abed."

"I'm sorry," Andrew said. "We would offer to return later, but I fear our circumstances are rather urgent, too."

"Always are. As long as you have the fee, Mr. Rickert will be up and about in a trice." She named a nominal sum for cost of the ceremony, which he readily retrieved from a pocket and gave to her.

"I'll fetch him for you now." She disappeared into the rear rooms of the cottage.

Miranda attempted to smooth her hair and her

travel-rumpled skirt. "I must look a fright—not what I would have wanted for our wedding."

Actually, her slightly mussed appearance excited him. He couldn't wait to see her thoroughly tousled. "You look more beautiful than ever."

She started to smile, then bit her lip. "Dash it. We don't have rings. I suppose we won't need them here, but we must get them as soon as possible. I want everyone who sees us to know that we're married."

"I have rings," Andrew said, slightly shy about admitting it. He fished two matching silver bands out of his vest pocket and showed them to her. "These belonged to my grandparents."

"They're perfect." She took the man's band and studied the Celtic knot design engraved on it. Grinning broadly, she met his gaze. "Does this mean I wasn't the only one hoping for an elopement?"

"Frankly, I didn't have much hope—but, yes, it's what I wished would happen."

She slipped into his arms and kissed him again. They were tangled in an embrace when the front door opened. Too engrossed in each other to be startled, they slowly pulled apart and looked to the newcomer.

Julian stood at the threshold, his arms crossed over his chest. "I thought I'd find you here."

"No," Miranda said softly. She moved closer to Andrew, clinging to his arm.

Andrew swallowed. "So you're the one who's been following us."

His cousin stepped inside and closed the door behind him. "Surely you didn't think I'd allow you to abduct my intended bride without a chase."

A sick dizziness spun through Andrew's head. He would *not* come this close to marrying Miranda, only to lose her in the end. If need be, he would fight his cousin until one of them collapsed—and he vowed he wouldn't be the one.

"Here I am," another masculine voice called from the rear of the cottage. A stout white-haired man with spectacles entered the room, the female servant following him. "Ah, you've brought a witness. That will save some time. Mrs. Chalmers here can serve as the second."

"I'm afraid this man's not likely to stand up for us," Andrew said through tight lips. He watched his cousin, expecting Julian to lunge at him any time.

Julian stared back, his face stony. After a moment, he blinked and turned away. Taking a deep breath, he stepped into the center of the room and looked at Mr. Rickert. "What the hell. I'll stand up for them."

Andrew frowned, confused by the turnaround. "I'm sure you didn't chase us all night just to witness our wedding."

His cousin met his gaze with a grimace. "No, but riding all night by oneself gives one plenty of time to think—something I likely don't do often enough. Being jilted is bloody humiliating, but I recognize that some of the blame lies with me. Besides, it would be no less humiliating to insist Miranda marry me when you've probably already tumbled her last night, if not on May Eve."

Andrew clenched his fists, but Miranda grabbed his arm and held him tightly.

She turned to Julian and lifted her chin. "*Several* times on both occasions, actually."

Andrew's gaze shot to her, his mouth open in shock.

She looked at him and smiled faintly.

He understood. It might be best to let Julian believe what he did.

Mr. Rickert cleared his throat. "Perhaps we'd better get on with the ceremony."

"Yes." Julian gave Andrew and Miranda a wry look. "Unless you want to wait for the bride's father to arrive. He shouldn't be far behind me."

They exchanged worried glances. Andrew didn't trust his cousin's motives, but there might not be time to locate another witness. He turned to Mr. Rickert. "Let's make haste, please."

"Of course." The man stepped up in front of them. "By Scottish law, you need only plight your troth before us and swear there are no impediments to your marrying. Then we'll all sign the register, and the marriage will be recorded."

Andrew took Miranda's hands in his and looked into her eyes. Unwilling to waste time worrying about phrasing, he stated his vows as simply as he could. "I take thee for my wife, Miranda Granville, and plight my troth to you for as long as we both shall live."

She gulped and smiled. "I take thee, Andrew Owen, for my husband, and plight my troth to you for as long as we both shall live."

"Do you swear there are no impediments to your marrying?" Mr. Rickert asked.

"I swear," they said in unison.

"I pronounce you man and wife." He gestured toward a large leather-bound ledger on a desk in the corner. "You first, Mrs. . . . . er, what was it?"

"Owen," Miranda said, already picking up a quill. She inked her name quickly and handed the quill to Andrew.

He scribbled in the space provided for the groom,

then looked to Julian, still nervous that his cousin had a trick up his sleeve.

His expression blank, Julian took the quill and signed—his real signature, Andrew noted. Julian passed the quill to Mrs. Chalmers. While she wrote in the ledger, he turned to Andrew and extended his hand. "Congratulations."

Andrew shook his cousin's hand, swallowing against a lump in his throat. "Thank you."

"Naturally, you'll want to consummate the marriage as soon as possible," Mr. Rickert said with no hint of embarrassment as he added his signature to the register. "No chance of anyone questioning its validity that way. My sister runs an inn just next door, and her rates are very reasonable."

Andrew looked at Miranda.

She smiled.

"Go on then," Julian said. "When Sir Wilfred arrives, I'll pass along your regrets—and show him the register."

For the first time in what seemed like ages, Andrew smiled at him. "Thanks, Cuz."

Then he took Miranda's hand and ran next door. When Mr. Rickert's sister appeared at the desk, he had his money out, ready to pay up front.

Within five minutes, they had a room.

SORROW'S
WEDDING

DONNA SIMPSON

CHAPTER ONE

Sorrow Marchand tugged a brush through her glossy blond curls as she sat at her dressing table and stared absently into the mirror, listening to the pacing outside her bedchamber door. In less than one month she would be married. She had attended the London Season as the guest of her honorary aunt, Lady Spotswycke, and had caught the eye of a very eligible beau, the Honourable Mr. Bertram Carlyle, had been wooed, courted, asked, and had accepted his offer of marriage.

The pacing outside of her bedchamber increased in speed, and she smiled at the sound. When the pacer could no longer bear to keep her thoughts to herself she would burst in.

Marriage. She had her parents' excellent example, and felt confident of her decision. She was nervous, but not unduly so. Bertram was everything he should be, and perhaps more than he knew. They would be happy together, at least most of the time; she was convinced of it.

Finally, the pacer burst into her room and flung herself down on the stool beside Sorrow.

"My dear," Sorrow's adopted mother said, "are you sure about everything? And have you . . . have you told Mr. Carlyle?"

Composed—unnaturally so, some in London had cruelly said—for so young a woman, not yet twenty-one, Sorrow turned on her seat and gave her mother a quick hug. "Mama, I'm sure. And he is Bert, not 'Mr. Carlyle.' He will be your son in just three weeks."

Mrs. Marchand worried at her lip with her teeth. "But have you told him?" she finally said.

Sorrow set her ornate silver brush aside on the mahogany dressing table. "Told him what?"

"About us."

"Of course I have. I told him about you and Father and how dear you both are and how much he will love you when he comes to know you."

The older woman's brow wrinkled into furrows, and she said, "No, Sorrow dear, don't avoid the subject. I meant have you told young Carlyle about . . ."

A keening moan outside the door stopped them both, and then a thudding noise, followed by the bump-bump-bump of something—or someone—falling or jumping down the stairs echoed through the old house. Sorrow and her mother both listened, heads cocked, eyes unfocused.

When there was no further outcry, Sorrow murmured, "It must be all right this time; if Joshua were hurt there would be such a ruckus."

"Don't avoid the subject, my dear. Have you told your future husband about us . . . about how we live? It is only fair that he should know what he is marrying into."

With the perpetually sunny smile that belied her somber name, Sorrow took her mother's hands in hers and rubbed them. "Mama, don't worry, please. Bertram is an excellent young man, very compassionate, good, sweet-natured, and with a sense of humor. He will not be alarmed. Once you meet him you'll understand."

"I wouldn't be so sure of that," Mrs. Marchand said, squeezing her daughter's hand.

"But you don't know him, Mama," Sorrow said, her oval face set in a most serious expression. "Do you think I would have said yes to his proposal if I was not absolutely sure?"

"But you should have warned him, should have explained . . ."

"No," the young woman said, holding up one hand. "No, please don't say I should have alerted him what to expect. There is no way to describe our life to someone who has never been here, never met you and Papa and the others. In words it sounds . . . oh, ludicrous. Impossibly senseless. Absurd. But in truth it is so lovely and simple and perfect. So don't say I should have warned him. I could never explain. And if I thought an explanation was necessary, then I never would have said yes to him."

"I will trust your judgment, my dear. But what shall you do if he decides he simply cannot face living as we do?"

"I believe in Bertram, Mama," she said, looking at her mother with a serene expression. "It will never come to that."

Another noise arose in the hall, and someone rapped on Sorrow's door.

"Mrs. Marchand, Mr. Howard is having a bad turn, ma'am, an' I'm not quite sure what to do."

"I am coming, Letty," Mrs. Marchand said, rising from the dressing table stool. Sorrow started to rise, too, but her mother pushed her back down and said, "No, dear, you stay here. I want you to get a goodly amount of sleep tonight. I would not have you looking haggard for your Bertram. He arrives early, I imagine, if he is a proper young bridegroom."

She exited the room and Sorrow picked up the

brush again, brushing her hair until sparks crackled and glittered in the dim reflection, all that could be seen by candlelight. Despite her calming words to her mother, she did feel a momentary qualm. For one thing, Bert would not be early, she was sure of it. He was a very diffident young man in many ways, and not as eager for this marriage as her mother seemed to think.

He would arrive by luncheon, perhaps, or later.

And then, though she never would have worried her mother with it, doubt assailed her in the dimness of her room. What if she was wrong? What if Bert was horrified by her life and her unusual family?

Then he was not the man she thought he was, she decided, laying the brush down again and crossing the bare wood floor to her bed. And she would not have him at any price, if that was the case. She snuffed her candle and snuggled under the covers. Down the hall, even through the heavy wood door, she could hear her mother singing a piece from an opera, her sweet, high voice fluting through the early summer night air and no doubt comforting poor Mr. Howard.

If Bertram could not see how beautiful her life at the Marchand home, Spirit Garden, was, then he would never understand her, nor what she wanted from life. And if that was true, he was not the man she suspected he was beneath his layers of London conventionality and they had no business marrying. It would be cold comfort, though, to know that he was not the right husband for her, when she did so look forward to their lives together.

But she would worry about that on the morrow. She closed her eyes, determined to sleep.

* * *

The Kent countryside was bursting with blooms in the hedgerows, and the early morning sun was raising a mist off the damp grass. It hovered, giving an eerie impression of phantoms undulating over the meadows. Bertram Carlyle was happy he had decided to ride down, sending his luggage and valet ahead of him, despite his father's recommendation that for the dignity of his position he ought to arrive at the Marchand estate—the oddly named Spirit Garden—by carriage. Defying his father never came easy, but in this case victory had come a little too effortlessly.

He suspected that his father, the very elegant and lordly Viscount Newton, didn't really believe that anything could make his only son dignified or welcome, even at his future bride's home.

Chastising himself for such a disloyal thought, Bertram finally rounded the curve in the road and saw before him the promised view of Spirit Garden.

Sorrow had told him it was the most beautiful place on earth, and with the song of the lark fluting through the June air, the scent of hedge roses in his nostrils, and the knowledge in his heart that Miss Sorrow Marchand had actually said yes to his proposal, he had to agree with her assessment.

It was a long, low house, three stories but seeming to melt into the Kentish countryside. Occupying a meadow near a stream, there were willows sweeping the waterway and a long green sward of grass swooping up to the house itself, interrupted only by a white crushed-limestone drive that circled in front of the manse. Beyond, barely visible, was a tiny chapel, the chapel where he and Sorrow Marchand would be wed in just over a fortnight.

The thought unnerved him.

He turned his gaze back to the main house. Gardens surrounded the building, and a kitchen garden behind filled the space from house to stable with fat cabbages and other greenery impossible to identify. Even from a distance he could see the early morning activity: a maid hanging laundry in a yard behind the house, another carrying pails of something from the house to a low piggery far from the stable, and a groom currying a horse in a paddock.

He pulled his mount, Tiberius, to a halt on a rise above the lane toward the house and waited, expecting doubt, fear, and dread to assail him, but, oddly, his heart did not thud, nor did his stomach clench. Every bridegroom should be nervous, should he not, at the thought of meeting his future parents-in-law? One would almost think he was coming home, that mythic place of welcome of which he had oft heard but never visited. Newton Castle only ever inspired loathing and illness in him, but in coming to Spirit Garden he felt a calmness overtake him.

It was most disquieting.

It was frightfully early, and he wondered if he ought to linger awhile, waiting until he could be sure his bride and her parents were awake and arisen. But no, there would be servants, and he could wait in a library or den, surely.

Taking a deep, bracing breath of Kentish air, he determined that he would not start this new relationship by being fearful and doubting. He had done that his whole life and he would not continue. It was unmanly. He was going to be a husband soon, and if he was fortunate, a father. A father should be confident, bold, strong . . . everything that was not him, in other words.

And if he was not careful, pessimistic, gloomy thoughts would darken this glorious spring day, and he would not allow that. He was sure that would come soon enough, when his father joined them to plan and execute the wedding, which was to take place at Spirit Garden not quite three weeks hence.

He set Tiberius to gallop and the gelding obliged, so two minutes saw him and his lathered mount arriving at the home of his intended bride. As he pulled his steed to a halt on the crushed limestone gravel, an ancient hound turned its sightless eyes toward Carlyle and bayed, head thrown back in ululating welcome.

Carlyle dismounted, disconcerted, and even more so when an elderly groom who, oddly, seemed to have only one arm, trotted out from behind the house and took Tiberius's bridle, leading the steed away as he said over his shoulder, "They're awaitin' ya, mister . . . jist go on in."

The hound left with the groom, his job apparently done. Carlyle gazed up at the staid house, larger and grander now that he was in front of it, and took a deep breath, but before he could mount the steps up to the front door, said door burst open and a stout young boy with a round face boiled from the house like a bee from a disturbed hive. He was howling incoherently and clutching his head. After him an older man in just a shirt and breeches, no coat or cravat, followed, hollering as he waved scissors, "Joshua, you *must* have your hair cut! You know I will not hurt you!"

The man skidded to a halt on the limestone drive at the sight of Carlyle. "Hello. You must be Bertram. Please go in. Mrs. Marchand and Sorrow are both about somewhere. Excuse me, but I must find Joshua. His hair is wet and I do not wish him to catch a cold." With that he bolted after the young fellow.

Carlyle stood staring after them. A woman came to the open door, glanced out, caught sight of him, and said, as she descended, "Oh, good heavens. Mr. Car-

lyle, is it? I told Sorrow you would be early, but she was
so sure you would not that I trusted her judgment,
when I should have trusted my own knowledge of how
a prospective bridegroom would behave. I felt certain
you would be eager to arrive and see Sorrow again."

"Mrs. Marchand?" he said, moving forward on
wooden legs and thrusting his hand out.

"Yes, of course! How good of you to come to us,
Mr. Carlyle, and how much we look forward to getting to know you. Please do not mind Mr. Marchand;
he has been trying to get Joshua to allow him to cut
his hair, and really, the boy badly needs a haircut, but
he will trust no one but my husband right now because he was so badly treated . . ."

She was still talking, her voice becoming muffled,
as she enfolded him in a fierce hug, something he
was not prepared for. He didn't even know the
woman! And that was Mr. Marchand, the coatless,
cravatless man following the howling boy? And who
was this Joshua? Was it Sorrow's . . . brother?

"Mama, Letty tells me that Tony told her that a
man had arrived on horseback. I said that it could
not be true, but she insisted . . ."

Carlyle, emerging from the embrace, looked up at
the house to see Miss Sorrow Marchand, his bride-to-
be and inhabitant of this strange house, daughter to
this woman who had just hugged him so ardently.

She was every bit as lovely as he remembered—
they had parted weeks ago, and he was beginning to
doubt his memory of her—blond and lithe, lively
and pert. She saw him, too, and her alabaster cheeks
pinkened.

His breath caught in his throat. He had forgotten.
In that moment he realized that he had forgotten
how much he liked her, how at ease he felt in her
company, and how very beautiful he thought she

was, though most in their London circle damned her faintly as "tolerable." He could not say he loved her, but then he knew she did not love him, either. He had no doubt that he was just the most acceptable alternative, as the future Viscount Newton, to life as a spinster. That she was twenty-one, almost, and unmarried, had seemed strange to him until he talked for a while with her and found that her manner of speaking some would call bold. Some whispered, too, that her family was eccentric, but until this very moment he had thought that perhaps meant they did not go out in company much. Now he wondered.

And yet . . . he was still very happy to see her.

"Bertram," she gasped, and clutched her hands in front of her.

"Sorrow," he said, smiling up at her, her mother still on his arm.

"Come in, come in," Sorrow said, pushing the door behind her open again.

"Welcome to Spirit Garden," Mrs. Marchand said, and mounted the steps with him.

CHAPTER TWO

They entered, Carlyle not sure, after such a strange greeting, what to expect. But the entrance was lovely, serene, with spring flowers in heavy urns and sunlight from sparkling windows touching the pale walls and gilt framed portraits.

Everything was elegant, calm, and decorous, including his bride-to-be and her mother.

"Your luggage and man arrived yesterday, Mr. Carlyle," Mrs. Marchand said over her shoulder.

"Bertram, please, ma'am. I *am* to be your son!" Even as he said it, he realized that it sounded terribly stuffy coming from him. But the words must stand as he said them.

"Of course," Mrs. Marchand said. "Bertram! Sorrow has told me I must call you that, and it's a lovely name, so . . ."

They were interrupted by a ghostly girl dressed all in gray who flitted into the hallway just before they reached a large door, half open, through which Bertram could see a parlor.

The girl wrung her hands together, rolling them over and over each other. "I can't get them clean! What am I to do? Sorrow, come help me; I can't get them clean!" Her whispered lament echoed against the high ceilings.

Sorrow immediately approached the girl and took her hands up in her own. "Margaret, your hands are clean, dear. Look at them; they're spotless."

"B-but they're not, and I've washed and I've washed and I can't seem to . . . the water's not hot enough, and the maid won't bring me any more and . . ."

Carlyle gazed at the girl, and then looked down at her hands, which Sorrow had captured and held still, though they still moved like restless kittens, independent of their owner. Margaret, as Sorrow had named her, stilled and gazed down at her own hands, which were red and chapped, blistered in spots.

Sorrow caught her mother's eye. "She was doing so well before today. I should go and talk to her, Mama; you know it is just all of the activity in the household that has brought this on."

"No, dear," Mrs. Marchand said in gentle tones, going to her daughter and taking the other young woman's arm. "Margaret must become accustomed to my help. You'll be going away and I must learn for myself what soothes her anxiety."

Nodding reluctantly, Sorrow released the girl but looked into her eyes. "Margaret," she said, softly, much as one might speak to a frightened puppy, "you know we spoke of this. Your hands are clean; it is just in your worry that you think they aren't. Let my mama help you."

Margaret nodded reluctantly and Mrs. Marchand guided the young woman toward the stairs to the upper floors. Over her shoulder she said, "Take Mr. Carlyle . . . er, Bertram . . . into the parlor, and I shall rejoin you presently."

Bertram followed Sorrow into a sunless room that, oddly, had a fire lighted already, so early in the day. She closed the door behind them.

"Should we not leave that open?" he asked. "I know we are engaged, but propriety . . ."

"Mr. Howard is here," she said, indicating a Bath chair close to the fire.

And indeed there was an ancient man in the chair, his eyes closed, his hands laying on his lap on top of a warm cover knit of soft blue wool.

Bertram stared at the man for a moment, but could detect no rise and fall of his chest, no sign that he was alive. "Is he . . . all right?"

"Yes, I imagine," Sorrow said. She moved over, stood close the man for a moment, and then nodded. "Yes, he's just sleeping. Poor Mr. Howard; he had a bad night last night and didn't sleep much, I think. Sometimes he sleeps better down here, by the fire."

"Who is he? He's not your grandfather or anything, or you would not call him Mr. Howard."

"No," she said, guiding Bertram to a settee by a window that was open a couple of inches. "He is no relation at all."

"Then . . ." Carlyle shook his head. "Why is he here?"

Sorrow looked uncomprehending. "Oh, you mean why are we looking after him and not some relative of his?"

Carlyle nodded.

A dark expression of anger passed over Sorrow's lovely face, but then was gone in a flash; so brief it was that he might have imagined it. "His nephew was going to put him in an asylum, for there was no one else to look after him. Luckily the young man's wife—little more than a girl, she is, but with a conscience—appealed to Mama for help. Papa and Mama invited him to come live with us."

Turning this over in his mind, Bertram shrugged,

finally, and looked up into Sorrow's eyes. She was watching him intently, he realized, and had been for a while. It was an expression he had noted on her face during their courtship. He often felt that she was trying to look *into* him, rather than *at* him, as odd as it sounded. He smiled at her and took her hands in his. "How lovely it is to see you again, Sorrow. I feel as if we parted so very long ago, but it's just a few weeks."

She sighed. "Yes, I've felt that too. I . . . I'm sorry you had such an odd welcome to Spirit Garden."

"Odd? Now what was odd about that? I have often heard of grooms being greeted at their fiancées' homes by their future fathers-in-law chasing young gentlemen in only their shirt and breeches."

Sorrow giggled.

Moved by an urge, Bertram leaned forward and kissed her swiftly on the mouth.

Though startled, his future wife did not shy away, but rather kissed him back, just as quickly and just as decisively. He rather liked it.

Conversation followed expected lines for a while, she asking about his trip down to Kent, and he asking how arrangements for their wedding were going. When, finally, the conversational stream slowed, he remembered a discussion they had in London and a promise she had made.

"I say, Sorrow, do you remember the night at the Lange ball? We sat in the conservatory for a while and I asked you about your name because it was so pretty but so sad, and you promised that when I came to Spirit Garden you would tell me the story of how you came to be named so."

"I remember."

"Tell me now," he said, taking up her hand and sitting back on the settee. He had often just watched her face, even when they were apart. He thought that though there were many prettier girls in London, there was not one whose face intrigued him more. She kept secrets, he thought, and yet told more truth than any girl he had ever met. A few gentlemen who had been attracted to her at one time or another complained that she had a way of looking at a man that made him feel she knew more about him than his own valet.

And yet, she would say or do something the next moment that would be completely naive. He liked that. It made him feel that marriage would be a voyage of discovery, not a lifetime anchored in port.

"All right." She sat back, gazed down at their joined hands, and said, "Bertram, I must preface my story by saying that I hope you will not feel I have held anything back, anything that you needed to know before asking me to marry you."

A jolt of trepidation coursed through him. "What is it?" Was there insanity in her family? He had forgotten Joshua and Mr. Marchand and their mad dash through the door as he arrived. Was that a part of her story?

"I am adopted," she said, without meeting his gaze. "The Marchands are not my real parents, though they adopted me when I was just days old."

He actually felt a thread of relief. He squeezed her hand. "It matters not a whit, my dear."

"Thank you for that; you're very kind. I know it would matter to many men. But there is more."

"I'm listening."

Sorrow gazed at him and saw in his eyes only kindness and compassion. It was what had drawn her to him in London, the feeling that beneath his stuffy layer of London conventionality there beat the heart of a compassionate and benevolent soul.

On an impulse, she said, "Bert, you are so good and kind . . . you didn't affiance me just out of that kindness, did you? I mean, I remember the night we met, that fellow—I don't remember his name—was making a cruel joke at my expense and you came to my rescue."

"No," he said, threading his fingers through hers. "My father had already decided you were suitable . . ."

Sorrow felt her heart clench; she didn't want to know that.

"But," he continued, "I never would have followed his recommendation if I had not seen you and thought that you were the loveliest girl I had seen for some time, and . . . and that there was something more to you than the other girls."

Examining his face in the dim light from the fire, she saw only honesty. "But you *had* asked other girls to marry you before."

He sighed. "I know. Please, Sorrow, don't hold that against me. If it counts for anything, I'm very happy they said no, now, because I am so very glad you said yes."

"It does count," she said, on a sigh. She held his hand up to her cheek for a moment, and then let their joined hands fall back to the bench

"Tell me the rest. You said there was more. And you still have not explained your name."

Sorrow settled back and felt Bertram's other arm around her back, touching her tentatively. It felt . . . comforting and yet somehow pleasantly agitating at the same time. "Papa . . . my papa now, that is . . . was a very wild young man. He and Mama lived a gay life—they had discovered that they could not have children, and decided that they should just enjoy themselves—but once, when Papa was racing along the road in the dark, his carriage went off into a ditch. It was a terrible accident and he almost died, for he hit his head on a rock."

"That's terrible!"

"Yes, but he was . . . he believes he was visited, as he clung to life, by a spirit that told him that in exchange for living, he must perform acts of charity. When he told Mama about this, though she took it quite seriously, so grateful was she that he had lived, they just didn't know what it meant."

Sorrow glanced up at her fiancé to see how he was taking her story. He was frowning, but it was an expression of concentration. He was not making fun of her, and that was good.

"And then they met my mother."

He nodded encouragingly.

"They already knew her family, but she was rumored to have run away to get married and had come to a bad end. She was destitute when Papa found out about her living in a sponging house in an awful part of London. She had married—she swore she truly had—and her husband had died, but her family didn't believe her and would not accept her because she was . . . she was carrying me."

Bertram sighed and looked very serious, but still said nothing.

"So Papa brought her home and told Mama he thought that he knew what the spirit meant. They talked about all the times they had seen something or heard something about someone in need and done nothing. The spirit simply meant they should do something. So they nursed my mother, but she died just a day after I was born, despite finally having a physician's aid. The last word she said was 'sorrow,' so that is what they named me. People talked. They said my mother was Papa's cast-off mistress and that

Mama was a fool for allowing it, but they didn't care; they adopted me."

She stopped and waited, not daring to look at Bertram, so it came as a complete surprise when he folded her into his arms and held her close.

"Sorrow, don't tell me you were afraid to tell me this in London?" he said, his voice hovering somewhere over her ear.

"I didn't know . . . I wasn't sure . . ."

He held her away from him and stared into her eyes. "You must never be afraid to tell me anything again. We are going to be man and wife. I . . . I care for you, Sorrow, and I want you to be happy."

"Oh, Bert, I knew you were the right one!" She threw her arms around him happily and kissed him, discovering, as she did so, that she was rewarded by a warm feeling that trickled through her.

Awkward at first, Bert became rather good at kissing her after a minute or two, and she happily settled into his arms, feeling his soft lips covering her cheeks and chin, nose and mouth, and his warm breath in her ear.

"Sorrow," he murmured, "I cannot believe . . ."

But whatever he couldn't believe was interrupted as the door was flung open and her Papa stood on the threshold, proudly escorting Joshua, duly shorn and pink from scrubbing.

"We have done it," her Papa said, "and have even come to see Sorrow's young man, haven't we, Joshua?"

The boy bobbled his head in a shy nod.

Behind him Margaret followed, calmer once more, and Sorrow's mama, too. She was followed by Letty, the maid, who carried a tray and complained, "If folks will move, a body could bring in the tray! Mr. Howard is needin' his tea!"

Sorrow shrugged and turned to Bertram, who was looking a little dazed by the onslaught of people bustling into the room. She bit her lip. "I don't think I finished explaining, Bert," she said. "There are more, but some are in their own rooms, and some don't rise until later. You'll meet everyone before tonight . . . or almost everyone, anyway. And if not tonight, then at breakfast tomorrow."

"Everyone?" he said, faintly.

"Everyone," she said, nodding firmly.

CHAPTER THREE

"Mr. Carlyle is very handsome," Margaret whispered to Sorrow as they did their evening check on two of the old dears.

"Do you think so?" Sorrow asked, creeping into one of the small quiet rooms on the third floor ahead of Margaret. She approached the bed, checked the bedside table for water and handkerchiefs, and watched old Mrs. Mackintosh sleep for a moment.

"I do."

"One of my friends in London damned his looks and said his ears stuck out too much."

"Then she was a great ninny," Margaret said, brushing back a strand of the old woman's hair and bending over her with a smile. She laid a kiss on the old woman's forehead and straightened. "And she did not know a gentleman when she saw one."

Arm in arm, they moved on to the next room, where an even older lady lay, close to death. She was so old that she had outlived the family who had cared for her before their own death, and so had needed a place to go. Letty was there, sitting by the bedside with her basket of darning, and Sorrow and Margaret held a whispered conference with her, asking after Miss Chandler. She was the same, Letty said, quiet, still breathing. She might have hours left or she might have months. The doctor was coming to see her on the morrow.

Sorrow thanked Letty for her care, and she and Margaret crept out, closing the door behind them. Servants did the actual labor involved in caring for the most elderly of the inhabitants of Spirit Garden, and a couple had evolved into fine nurses, especially Letty, for all her complaining. But Sorrow or her mother checked on all of their friends every day a few times, and arranged special treats, taking those able outside when the weather permitted. Sorrow had determined not to let her own impending nuptials change her habits, for she knew the old folks would miss her when she left. Margaret was starting to take an interest and that was good, for it was the best cure for her own problems, Sorrow had learned; it made her think about others instead of her own fears and worries.

In the hall once again, Sorrow said, "I agree. Bertram is very good looking, and he kisses wonderfully!"

"Kisses? He has kissed you?" Margaret gasped, and then dissolved into giggles.

They retreated to Margaret's room, her haven, she called it, the walls covered with her sensitive and brilliant watercolor paintings. She could not bear to wear bright colors, preferring gray or brown, but her paintings were always filled with beautiful hues. Sorrow saw a new one and exclaimed over it. "Oh, Margaret! It's . . . it's beautiful!"

It was quite obviously of herself and Sorrow was deeply touched. Margaret, when she was calm, painted quite lovely works, but, oddly, it was when she was disturbed and at her most agitated that she painted with a brilliance and intensity that was frightening, the colors deeper, the images more vibrant, but sometimes hard to understand. This was clearly painted in one of her sunny moods and showed Sorrow in a white lace gown holding a bouquet of roses. She reached out and hugged Margaret to her.

"It is to be a wedding gift for you and Mr. Carlyle," the girl said, shyly. "I hope to do one of him to match, now that he is here."

Overcome by a sudden case of nerves, Sorrow sat down on Margaret's narrow bed and covered her face with both hands. "Am I doing the right thing? Will he ever understand me?"

Margaret sat down by her and said, "What's wrong? Do you not love him? Isn't he perfect?"

Struggling to put her fears into words, Sorrow uncovered her face and said, "Perfect? Well, no. He's a little stuffy and too diffident. He's a very intelligent young man, but he lets his father rule him. Will that continue? And what about his father? I only met the man three times, but I quite despise him. Will Bertram understand that?"

"I had been thinking marriage was a solution to all a lady's problems," Margaret admitted, with a rueful tone, "but it seems that it creates quite as many as it solves."

Turning on the bed and drawing one leg up under her, Sorrow said, "Please, Margaret, don't mistake me. I still want to marry Bert. He's a good man, better, I think, than he even realizes, or I should not be marrying him. I . . . I care for him a great deal. Shall I tell you how I first saw him?"

Margaret nodded.

"He doesn't even know this," Sorrow said, twisting her hands together and staring off at one of Margaret's paintings on the wall. "But I first saw Bertram at a dinner party at the home of friends of my aunt, Lady Spotswycke. I had wandered off to the library—out of boredom, I'm afraid, for there were a great many pompous people there—when I heard an argument. I came out to the hall and saw a young man abusing a maid. I was about to make my presence known when Bertram came out of the drawing room, assessed the situation immediately, stopped the fellow, and shamed him into apologizing—actually apologizing!—to the poor maid. I was immensely impressed—even more so when I found out later that he had escorted the poor girl to the butler and demanded she have a few moments and not be expected to wait upon that young man again. And even *more* so when I discovered he had spoken to the hostess to make sure the girl did not suffer, for a maid will often be dismissed for that kind of thing, you know, and who knows what the young man who abused her would say about her to her employer?"

Margaret, listening intently, said, "Why have you not told Bertram about this? Witnessing this?"

"It was a private deed, and he would be embarrassed if I told him what I saw and how affected I was by his kindness and consideration."

"But . . ." Margaret hesitated, but then said, "You have not said you love him. Did you say yes to his proposal because he is kind? Are there not other kind men in London?"

"Of course." Sorrow gazed down, untwisted her hands, and plucked at the bedspread. "But Bert . . . I don't know how to explain it. He . . . captured me. I knew, somehow, that we could have a wonderful life together, and, Margaret, I want children and a home and . . . all the other things every lady wants."

Wistfully, Margaret said, "Do you think *I'll* ever have those things?"

Sorrow took her hands in her own. "I believe you can," she said, knowing of the girl's fears. "But you must give yourself time to learn how to calm yourself. You're a very special person and deserve everything in life, but you must give yourself time."

"You're right of course," Margaret said, softly, her voice breaking. "How can I think of marriage when I'm afraid even to leave Spirit Garden? If it was not for your parents, I don't know . . . I don't know if I would still be alive."

Sorrow took the girl in her arms. She had seen the cuts on Margaret's wrists when the girl first came, and knew that she had made a solemn promise to the Marchands never to do that again. She had been like a wounded bird, afraid to fly, but gaining strength and confidence slowly. "Give yourself time," Sorrow said, releasing her. "Even if you need to stay here forever . . ."

"No!" Margaret sat up straight. "I will be strong some day. Maybe soon. Sorrow, I have begun to feel, lately, that I might learn to make my own way. I want to go to London for a visit, and Mr. Marchand has promised I might go and visit Lady Spotswycke. And . . . may I come and stay with you and Mr. Carlyle when you are married? I mean, only for a week or so, and not right away . . ." She blushed and turned her face away. "I know you will want to be alone together for a while, but sometime?"

"Of course," Sorrow said, pulling her friend back into a hug. "Of course you may."

Bertram stood outside the library door, knowing Mr. Marchand was in the library going over some estate papers. He wanted to talk to him but wasn't sure what he would say. He had so many questions about the day, and about the Marchands. Their household was unlike any he had ever visited, seeming almost like a hospital at times, and at others like the most joyous family home one could imagine.

This visit had started oddly and showed no sign of ever being normal. Dinner had been served in a series of fits and starts, with Mr. and Mrs. Marchand called away a couple of times to attend to emergencies. At that moment his fiancée, instead of being in the parlor playing the piano or netting a purse, was upstairs seeing to "the old folks," as she called them. It appeared that Mr. Howard was not the only elderly, sickly inmate of Spirit Garden.

Boldness. He was trying to cultivate a new attitude of boldness and courage, Bertram told himself, as he raised one hand and rapped on the door. At the summons, he entered.

The library was cluttered, with books over every surface. Mr. Marchand, oddly youthful even with his graying hair, sat on the floor among piles of books, cross-legged with one open on his lap. He looked up over his glasses and smiled. "Bertram! How good of you to visit me. Time we had a talk, eh?"

"Yes, sir," Bertram said, trying to think where he would sit, whether the man expected him to collapse onto the carpet with him, or should he be more dignified in talking to his future father-in-law?

"Take a chair, young man . . . just push those books to one side or pile them on the desk."

Bertram shifted a pile of books from a wing chair to a side table and sat down. "What are all these books, sir?"

Frowning down at the one in his hands, Mr. Marchand said, "They are medical books, such as they are, I suppose, on the state of the mind. You witnessed my tussle with young Joshua today . . ."

"Who is Joshua, sir? If I might ask?" After Sorrow's story he had some insight into Mr. Marchand, but was fascinated by what made such a man do what he did. Surely he had more than fulfilled the expectations any spectral being had of him in exchange for his life!

"Joshua is the son of a couple whose name you would recognize immediately, if I told you. Joshua is their youngest. He . . ." Mr. Marchand, his silver-tinged hair and silver-rimmed glasses glinting in the lamplight of his library, frowned down at the book in his hands again and then continued. "He is troublesome to them. He will allow only so much contact before he rebels and cannot bear to be touched or spoken to. I would not have chased him so this morning if his hair had not gotten into such a state. I have found that in most cases it does not help to force things on these folks." He paused and shook his head, and with a sad tone muttered, "They used to use ties to confine poor Joshua. It only made him afraid and wild. But he is getting better, though you would not know it by that spectacle this morning, eh?"

Bertram watched Sorrow's father, considering what she had told him of the man. He was as unlike Bertram's own father as two men could be, and he wondered what the two fathers would make of each other when Lord Newton arrived later in the week. But first he wanted to have some understanding himself, so he could try to explain this household and this family to his father.

He had no doubt that if Lord Newton had known the depths of the Marchands' eccentricity he never would have considered his son marrying into the family, but now that it was accomplished, now that he had Sorrow to plan for as his future wife, Bertram had no intention of giving her up for anything. The kisses they had shared that afternoon had left him strangely elated and with the oddest feeling of walking on clouds, and he wanted to feel that more and more often.

"Mr. Marchand, why do you do what you do? I mean . . . Sorrow has told me about . . . about her origin and how you came to adopt her, but why do you continue? Surely you have done enough good in your life and should enjoy your time, now."

The older man leaned back against the chair behind him and set aside his book. He took off his glasses and met Bertram's eyes for the first time. "In truth, when I started, though I felt much enthusiasm, I didn't know what I was doing. My only goal was to help people. Whoever needed it. But when I opened my eyes it was to see how terrible we are here in this country at looking after those who do not fit into our narrow strictures of proper behavior."

"Sir, pardon me for saying this, but . . . you don't really believe you were . . . were visited by a being or . . . or ghost, do you?"

"You are not so closed that you dismiss outright the possibility, are you?"

"Well, I suppose . . ."

"I don't know what happened that night. I don't think we know enough about the miracle that is our brain," Mr. Marchand said, tapping his head with one finger. "Did I invent the being to give myself hope and courage? Did it indeed give me the power to stay alive until help came? I was very badly hurt. Or was I indeed hovering between this world and the next? Do you claim, sir, to have a definitive answer to that which has plagued men for centuries?"

Bertram felt foolish, suddenly, even to question this man who had so clearly thought much on the topic. "No, sir, I would never dream of claiming some special knowledge."

"But you are allowed to doubt any part of my story. I was in a great deal of pain at the time and may have imagined the whole thing. However, regardless of the impetus, this . . . this way of living," the man said, waving his arms around to indicate the whole of Spirit Garden and all of its inhabitants, "has been a Godsend. I was aimless before, wandering, with no purpose, and a man without purpose is fulfilling only a particle of his function on earth. Just think of the possibilities," he said, leaning forward and tossing the book aside. "Just think, if every person who was able would do everything they could in life to better life for those around them . . . well, the world would be an astonishing place. No hunger, no pain . . . peace!" He sighed. "Formidable. It would be formidable, sir!"

His enthusiasm, while infectious, was frightening in its intensity and Bertram didn't quite know what to say. Was this what Sorrow expected of him? How could he ever measure up to her father, if that was so?

Would he be expected to fill his home with the ill and poor?

He didn't know if he could do it. And he was terribly afraid he would be disappointing Sorrow every day of their life together.

CHAPTER FOUR

If the whole of Spirit Garden disappeared in the morning mist it would leave the world impoverished, Bertram thought the next morning, as he took an early walk around the grounds. He looked up at the mellow brick and stone, ivy climbing the walls, roses beginning to bud against the stone fence, and wondered if that was what mankind had been placed on earth for, to help each other and learn that every person was so connected to the other that the pain of one impoverished the species.

And in the next moment he wondered what had infected him with such strange thoughts, for he had never before mused on the purpose of life.

A low fog gathered in the hollows of the meadow beyond the gardens. Through the fog he saw a woman, not young but not old, moving at a measured pace. She carried a basket filled with greens and seemed to be deep in concentration. When she looked up as she came to the garden gate, she stopped and gazed at him steadily for a long moment, no smile on her calm round face, and then said in a soft tone, "You must be Mr. Bertram Carlyle."

"You have the advantage of me, madam, for I don't know you."

She chuckled, fumbled with the gate latch, and nodded a thanks when he rushed to open it for her. "I know you by description. I arrived back at Spirit Garden late last night, coming back from the sickbed of an acquaintance."

"I hope you left your acquaintance better?"

"I did." She passed through the gate and took his offered arm.

She was a lovely woman in her forties, he thought, though he was no judge of age, and perhaps she was a relation. For she was not ill, nor was she deranged. She seemed calm and lovely and perfectly sane.

He guided her to the front door where she stopped and said, "Are you coming in to breakfast, sir?"

"In a moment. I was just . . . the garden is very peaceful in the early morning."

"And conducive to thinking," she said. She put out her right hand. "I am Mrs. Liston."

"Are you . . . are you related to the Marchands, ma'am?"

She smiled and looked up at the house. "Only by ties of the heart. They rescued me from . . . from penury or worse."

"Oh."

She met his gaze again. "Ah, you had hoped you had finally found one person here who was not one of their pensioners. That would not be me. I have much to be grateful for in life, chief among them the Marchands. You are getting a gem in Sorrow."

"I know it," Bertram said, turning away. "But what is she getting in me?"

"I beg your pardon? I did not hear the last part," she said, hand on the doorknob to go in.

"Nothing, ma'am," he said, turning back toward

her, ashamed of his muttering. "Please, do not let me keep you from your breakfast."

"Come in soon, Mr. Carlyle. You will be able to meet everyone that way."

"There are more than I have already met?"

"Yes, of course. There are always more, and the breakfast table is where we all meet. We have breakfast early here. Do come in soon."

She entered as Bertram watched. More. There were more people? Would Sorrow expect her life to be like this? Would she make of their home this . . . this madhouse? He was ashamed the next moment for thinking that way, but still could not erase his fears. He was not certain that he could manage a life like this, and surely that meant he was lacking in compassion or benevolence or something. Was he heartless? He had not been used to thinking so, but maybe he was.

But Sorrow . . . he had begun to think they were very well suited.

There was only one thing to do, and that was to talk to her about it.

He squared his shoulders and entered.

"Oh, Mrs. Liston, I'm so happy for you," Sorrow said, hugging the plump widow and patting at her tears. Sorrow's father had just told Mrs. Liston of the letter he got that finally guaranteed her her rightful widow's portion of her late husband's income. It was not a fortune, but it would allow her to live. "But does that mean you will be leaving us?"

"Yes, my dear, even as you will be leaving Spirit Garden. I met your young man outside as I came in. He seems very . . . nice."

Sorrow noted the reservation in the woman's tone

and the hesitation, and wondered what the lady had sensed to be lacking. Mrs. Liston, though, had suffered gravely at the hands of men and was not very trusting. Perhaps it was just that she didn't know Bertram yet.

Her fiancé at that moment entered the breakfast room and looked around at the gathering, a little bewildered. There were eight at the large round table, including Sorrow, Mrs. Liston, Sorrow's father, and Joshua. But there were also Margaret, of course, and three others.

Sorrow greeted him and said, "You know most of us, but there are also Nancy Smith, who comes up from the village every day to help us with the old folks," she said, indicating a shy, plump girl with a port wine birthmark that covered her cheek, "Billy, who only has breakfast with us"—she indicated a young legless boy in a Bath chair—"since he is too busy in the conservatory with the plants for the rest of the day, and Mr. William." She indicated the last man, a quiet older gentleman who made his way through a plate of eggs and herring, not seeming to notice the hubbub of the room.

"Mr. William?" Bertram gazed at the man, perhaps expecting an explanation.

Sorrow leaned toward her fiancé and whispered, "I will tell you about him later."

"Sit, Carlyle," Sorrow's father said, indicating the empty chair beside him. "We don't stand on ceremony for breakfast. You can see it is our largest meal. The rest of the day many have trays or just get something from Cook."

Mrs. Marchand entered just then. "Good morning, dearest," she said to Sorrow, giving her a hug. She dropped a kiss on her husband's silvered head and ruffled Joshua's hair and then Billy's.

Bertram was looking very pale and ate his breakfast in silence. Sorrow watched him.

Of all the men in London, he was the only one she thought might understand her family and their way of life. He was kind—she knew that already—but did have an unfortunate tendency toward stuffiness that she hoped was not inherent. She and her mother exchanged worried looks. This had been Mrs. Marchand's fear, that this prenuptial visit would frighten Bertram away. But Sorrow's reasoning still stood. There would have been no way to prepare him for her family life. It would have sounded like insanity.

In truth, it worked far better than anyone had a right to expect, but that was because over the years the Marchands had developed a tolerance for chaos. But Bertram, raised by the dignified, pompous Lord Newton in his quiet household and the hard discipline of good schools . . . how would he react?

After breakfast, she said, shyly, "Would you like to see my favorite spot on the estate?"

He nodded, still wordless, and she took his hand and led him outside, through the garden, out the gate, and across the long lawn that led down to the brook, toward an oak tree that stood in lonely majesty near the edge of the wooded copse that signaled the end of the Marchand property.

The early fog had burned off and it was a glorious June day with a sky so blue it hurt her eyes just to look. A light breeze ruffled her new gown, a pretty dotted lawn confection of pale rose and green. She thought she looked well enough in it, but wasn't sure the style suited her.

Finding a dress to suit her simple and specific tastes was almost as hard as finding a husband to suit her heart's desire. In London she had known from the beginning that she might never find a man who fit her needs and was also attracted to her. She had seen Bertram long before he appeared to notice her, but once he did, and made the attempt to get to know her, they had gotten on fine.

Perhaps that was why it had sorely disappointed her to hear that the impetus for Bertram to look in her direction had come from his father, but she stuffed back the doubt. Did it really matter how it had happened? It had, and she had liked him from the start, and had hoped he liked her just as much. There were far prettier girls in London, certainly, and though he had had a couple of disappointments in the past—his courting misadventures had been the gossip of their circle—she had paid the chatter no mind.

They finally stood in the shade of the oak tree. "Isn't it magnificent?"

He sighed. "Yes, I suppose."

"Let's sit down," she said, indicating the soft grass under the tree.

"But it is so damp! You will stain your pretty dress!"

"I don't care about that. Do . . . do you really like it? I wasn't sure . . ."

"It makes you look like a flower," he said, smiling finally. "It is almost pretty enough to do you justice."

She sighed happily. "You say such lovely things, Bert," she said, standing on tiptoe and kissing his cheek.

He took her in his arms and kissed her then, and she closed her eyes, surrendering to the sweetness of his mouth on hers, and the security of his arms around her. She put her arms around his neck and kissed him back, letting all of her hope and fear and longing pour out of her.

They sank down together and he pulled her close,

their bodies reclining in the shade of the tree and their mouths joined still, their breath mingling, their separateness melting away in the warmth of their joined heartbeats.

When he stopped kissing her and she opened her eyes, it was to find him staring down at her with a fierce, yearning hope in his gray eyes. She rested her head back on the comfortable firmness of his arm and reached up, pushing one lock of dark hair behind his ear. "Bert, what is it? I have been feeling . . . oh, I don't know. I've been worried, this morning. You seemed . . . different."

He pulled away from her and sat up, his elbows on his drawn-up knees. He stared down to the stream, glinting silver in the brilliant sunshine. When he glanced back at her, his doubtful expression melted into a smile.

"Whenever I look at you, I feel this . . . this surge of hope that we can work it all out."

"Work what out?"

"Our lives. Sorrow, we're so different, and our lives have been so different. What if . . . what if we want different things? We haven't even talked about that. You didn't tell me about any of this in London."

"This?"

"This! All of this, how your parents are, and how you were raised, all your . . . all the people!"

He sounded overwhelmed. She had to remind herself to allow for that. It all seemed so natural to her that she never understood other people's reactions. "Would you have understood if I had tried to explain?" She watched his eyes, the flickering emotions that changed them from dove gray to charcoal and the pupils from small to large.

"I don't know."

"And does it change who I am?"

He breathed in a deep sigh. At long last he said, "No. No, I don't suppose so. But it still doesn't mean that we understand each other." He reclined beside her and faced her, gazing into her eyes and tentatively reaching out to touch her cheek. "You are so pretty."

She rubbed her cheek against his hand. "I think you must care for me to say such a lovely thing, for I am nothing in looks compared to Lady Mary Rountree, the last girl you asked to marry you."

He flinched, and she was sorry she had said such a thing.

"Bert, I'm sorry! I don't know why I said that. I don't know . . ." She stopped and searched her heart. "That's not true. I do know. Bert, the other girls you asked to marry you were much prettier than I, but they said no. Did you ask me . . . did you just ask me because you thought I might say yes? I know that . . . I know that you have been wanting to marry these last two Seasons, and that you will come into your maternal inheritance when you do . . ."

"Stop," he said, putting his finger over her mouth. He leaned forward and kissed her. "I see we are to be honest with each other." He faced her, gazing down at her with a determined expression on his square face. "So I will tell you. At first I asked you because I thought you might say yes. You're almost twenty-one, and I thought . . . that is . . ."

"That you were my last chance?" She giggled and lay back, gazing up through the green leaves. She stretched and put her hands behind her head. "Oh, Bert, I do want to be married! But I would never have married just anyone. I love my life and my parents, and I'm happy enough most of the time." She looked back at him and was touched by the hope in his eyes. "Shall I tell you . . ." She sat up. "Bert, I saw you and liked you before you ever noticed me." She told him then the story of seeing him intercede for the poor maid at the dinner party.

He was silent. "I have to say, Sorrow, that . . . well, that was an aberration for me. I don't usually go out looking for maidens to save. It was just that Charles was being so beastly to that poor girl, and . . . but I'm not like your father, you know. I . . . I don't know if I ever could be."

It struck her then, that perhaps he thought she expected another man like her father. She didn't. She didn't even know if she necessarily wanted to live the same way as life was at Spirit Garden. That was what she hoped to discover with a man like Bert. She knelt in front of him and pulled him up. "Bert," she said putting her arms around his waist. "I don't need you to be a knight on a charger. I just want someone to care for me. And I don't plan to go looking for wounded spirits to save; I don't know what is in my future. I don't know if that is how we will live. That's something we'll decide together!"

He gazed down at her and his gray eyes gleamed in the filtered sunlight. "Sorrow, I . . . oh, Sorrow!"

He kissed her again, and together they tumbled to the ground in a storm of kisses and caresses. She felt every last barrier in her heart give way and knew then that she truly had fallen in love with Bertram Carlyle.

CHAPTER FIVE

Bertram and Sorrow walked back to the house arm in arm, with Sorrow leaning her head on his shoulder. Bertram thought he had never been so happy in his life, and the day had taken on a golden hue, with everything from the humblest rock and weed to the loveliest flower gilded.

Chance. It had all been chance that Lady Mary Rountree had not said yes, and the girl before her. Not a one of them could hold a candle to Sorrow Marchand, the prettiest, sweetest, loveliest girl in the kingdom.

He was a fortunate man and his life was going to be good. He looked forward to his nuptials now with an unreserved enthusiasm, knowing that he and Sorrow would be partners in life.

He strolled with her up the greensward and topped the rise to see a carriage drawn up to the house with the red and gold crest of the Newton coat of arms.

His father was there already, two days early. The golden day turned drab.

"It's your father, Bert! He's early. He must be looking forward to the visit!" Nothing could dim Sorrow's happiness that day, and she was determined to learn to like Bert's father, no matter how daunting that task seemed.

She pulled her fiancé forward. They approached the house to find that Lord Newton was overseeing the unloading of his carriage, and that he seemed to have brought enough trunks and valises to clothe several men for a stay of some months, instead of just one for about two weeks. She and Bert strolled up to the viscount.

"Bertram," the man said, with little enthusiasm. "Miss Marchand."

Sorrow, determined to be herself, threw her arms around Lord Newton and hugged him hard, then placed an exuberant kiss on his chilly cheek. "Father-to-be! Welcome to Spirit Garden."

"What kind of name is that for an estate?" he asked, disentangling himself from her embrace with firm hands.

"Well," Sorrow said, determined not to take offense, "my mama and papa didn't have a country estate when first they married. They had only a London home. But after Papa had an accident, and when I came along, they decided they wanted a home in the country, and this was it!" She swept a hand around indicating the entire estate. "It was vacant, and its history was very sad. The people who had owned it for a hundred years, their family . . ."

"Yes, yes, yes," Lord Newton said impatiently. "Bertram," he said, turning to his son, "have you told Miss Marchand that after you marry you will be expected to come back to Newton Castle for a formal reception? Miss Marchand's family is, of course, welcome, but by no means . . ."

The front door flew open just then and Joshua, pushing Billy's Bath chair, flew out the front door and down the steps with the chair-bound boy laughing merrily. Sorrow's father followed, gasping out, "Joshua, be careful, please! It could be dangerous, and I never intended you to go outside the house with young Billy! Please, son, be careful!" Mr. Marchand stopped and stared at the carriage. "Oh, good Lord, no one told us we had company."

As Lord Newton gaped, Sorrow's father stepped back to the front door and hollered, "Mother, we have company! I do believe it is Lord Newton, and he has brought more trunks than I have ever seen." His message delivered, he strode forward to the viscount, grabbed his hand, and pumped it vigorously. That action not enough for his overflowing bonhomie, he clasped the other man to him in a manly embrace. "Newton, good to meet you! Bertram is a wonderful lad, and we couldn't be prouder that our Sorrow has nabbed him."

Sorrow giggled. If she had hoped to see the stuffy Lord Newton deflated, she need only have imagined this meeting. The viscount was speechless. She glanced up at Bertram to see if he was enjoying the spectacle, but her fiancé was gaping, too, and looked alarmed.

Perhaps she ought to intervene.

"Lord Newton, you must be tired after your journey. I understand you have been back to Newton Castle in the interim, between London and here. Let me show you to your room." She took the viscount's arm and led him up the steps to the front door, but threw one look over her shoulder at Bert. He shrugged.

As they entered, Mrs. Marchand bustled forward in the hall with a worried expression. "My lord, welcome to Spirit Garden. I apologize for the informal welcome but, really, we didn't expect you for two more days."

Sorrow exchanged a glance with her mother, who had already expressed concern over how best to break to the viscount their original way of living. It appeared all their speculation was for naught, given his precipitate arrival.

Mr. Marchand was following them in with his arm around Bertram, who, with the arrival of his father, seemed to have pokered up into the stuffy fellow he often appeared to be in London. Sorrow felt rather as though she were in a careening carriage headed downhill with a lake at the bottom. There seemed to be no way to avert disaster, and she wondered if she ought even to try. If Bertram would let his father affect him still, at his age, then there was no hope he would behave like a man ought when married.

"Father, you should have sent a message ahead," he said, just as she was thinking that. "The Marchands have a busy household and would have appreciated word that you were coming early."

"Busy household? Does that include that mad child and the legless boy?" The viscount looked disgruntled and completely unaware of the silence that had fallen around him.

Bertram disengaged himself from his future father-in-law and confronted his father as the sunlit hall dimmed. "Yes, those children are a part of this household. I think you owe both the boys and the Marchands more respect when you address them."

The June day had turned chilly, even wintry, inside the normally warm and sunny home. Lord Newton bowed. "My most sincere apologies if I have offended anyone in saying only what appeared to be fact. I would like to rest in my room for an hour or so, if that is permitted."

"Certainly," Mrs. Marchand said, faintly. "I will have someone show you to your room."

* * *

It was a day of discovery for Bertram. He had barely found his own feet at Spirit Garden and wished his father hadn't come so quickly, but Lord Newton's arrival made him determined to meet all of the inmates of the home and make his own judgment as to how the Marchands lived.

His father was deeply offended by his reprimand and would likely stay in his room for the rest of the day, punishing all, he would reason, by depriving them of his lordly presence. So Bert, knowing that Sorrow had duties to attend to, volunteered to retrieve Joshua and Billy, first, and to make sure they had come to no harm.

He found them in the garden outside, with Joshua ambling aimlessly by the hedge and Billy tending as best he could to a topiary shaped like a . . . well, Bert couldn't quite tell what it was, but the boy was concentrating fiercely, snipping with precision and determination.

At breakfast he had noticed that Billy, though shy, was a normal ten-year-old boy in every other way but that he had been born with no legs. Bert approached him and said, heartily, "What are you doing there, young fellow?"

The boy, with a withering glance worthy of an adult, said, "I am trimming a bush."

Bert stifled a smile and sat down on the gravel path near the bush so he didn't hang over the child like a giant. This was clearly a lad to be taken seriously. "Ah, but you see it is clear you are meaning to make it a certain shape, but that shape is not obvious to me yet, dunce that I am, so you will have to tell me exactly what you are doing. There is a difference, you see, in what I meant and what you thought I meant."

Joshua, listening, hovered close by. He, on the other hand, Bert thought, was physically quite capable but did not like direct confrontation except with those with whom he was familiar.

Frowning, Billy said, "I am trying to make it into a dragon."

"A dragon?"

"Yes. A dragon flying. I saw one in a book."

"You mean like the one St. George killed?"

"That is just a legend," Billy said, snipping again, carefully. He regarded the bush. "I know people say dragons never lived, but . . . but how wonderful if it is true, and they really did fly!"

Bert's breath caught in his throat. To fly! How wonderful that must seem to a boy who never had the chance to even walk. "I think you were just about flying a while ago when Joshua was pushing your chair."

Billy's eyes gleamed and he shared a glance with Joshua, who chuckled to himself and danced away to torment a butterfly, chasing it about the garden. "He likes to push me about. I think . . . I think it makes him feel that he is like Mr. Marchand . . . you know . . . helping people."

Helping people. It seemed so simple, the way Billy said it. A shiver raced down Bert's back. He remembered his father-in-law's words the night before in the library, about how wonderful it would be if everyone in the world helped each other to the best of their abilities. A naive concept, his London friends would say. And yet, there was something to it. It seemed to grow from there, like an infection—only in a good way, leaping from one person to the next and inspiring hope and determination.

He gazed at the bush and began to see what Billy's careful snipping was achieving, branch by branch, cut by cut. There was a wing, and there the long extended neck, and behind, the beginning of a stubby tail. "I see it!" he said, and ran his hand over the wing. "This is the right wing of the dragon!"

"Yes," Billy said. "By autumn, I hope he is in full flight."

Bert clapped him on the shoulder. "I'm sure he will be, young man. I *know* he will be!"

Looking out an upstairs window as she passed from one room to the next, Sorrow spotted Bert in the garden with Billy and Joshua. He had his hand on Billy's shoulder and they were looking at the boy's topiary. Hope coursed through her. Maybe . . . maybe they would have a life together that would fulfill all her own dreams and perhaps even more. She had to believe in her intuition and believe in Bert.

Lord Newton stamped up the stairs at that moment. He stopped at the top and stared at her. "I was in my room, but there was a noise. I went to investigate, and what do I find but some . . . some relic of an ancient fellow having a nightmare in the middle of the day!"

"Oh dear," Sorrow said. "Was it poor Mr. Howard? Is there someone with him?"

"Yes, your mother came." Lord Newton approached and stared out the window, down at his son. "What on earth is Bertram doing out there? He is sitting on the ground!"

"Yes, with Billy. Isn't it marvelous?"

"No, it most certainly is not!" He turned to Sorrow. "Young lady, if I had known . . ." He shook his head and walked away, back to his room down the hallway.

Margaret, coming down the stairs from the third floor, watched him storm into his room and slam the door. "W-what is wrong with him? That is Lord Newton, isn't it? I s-saw him from the parlor earlier b-but I didn't come to meet him. What is wrong?"

Sorrow took her friend's arm and gave it a reassuring squeeze. "Nothing, really. He . . . he was just resting and Mr. Howard disturbed him with one of his nightmares. It's all right."

But try as she might to convince her friend, Sorrow had a foreboding feeling that Lord Newton's ire would not have a happy ending for any of them.

CHAPTER SIX

"How did I never hear of this?" Lord Newton said, pacing up and down in the cramped quarters of Mr. Marchand's library. He tripped over a heap of books and they slid sideways with a soft thump; he glared at them for a moment, then scowled down at his son. "How did I never hear that the Marchands gather every cripple, every dying old man or woman, every . . . every *idiot* into their household?"

Bert, sitting where he had to speak with Mr. Marchand the night before, gazed up at his father but did not respond. What should he say? What was there to say? Over his life Lord Newton had dominated him, he knew, but the viscount was an overwhelming obstacle once his ire was raised, and it had just been easier to go along with his father than fight him every inch of the way.

But something had changed, and an anger was building in Bert at the way his father was characterizing the Marchands, whom he had found to be charming, if eccentric, and welcoming in an oddly heartwarming way. Though their life was perhaps not one he would choose for himself every day, he respected their decisions and disliked hearing his father's demeaning assessment of their work.

Maybe there *was* something to say. He took a deep,

steadying breath. "Father, the Marchands are kind people and have dedicated their lives to helping people others ignore. I was . . . well, I was surprised at first myself, but I'm sure after you have spoken to some of the people and . . ."

"Nothing will change my mind," the viscount roared. "I am sorry now that I ever thought of Miss Marchand for you."

"And I'm ashamed that I didn't find her myself," Bert said, rising. "For though I had seen her, I paid her no mind until you pointed out that she was nearing one-and-twenty, of a tolerably good family, and single still. I'm a fortunate man that fate seems to have conspired to bring us together. That the Marchands rescued her mother and adopted her twenty years ago, and then that . . ."

"Adopted her? She is adopted?"

"Yes," Bert said. "Her mother died bearing her, and the Marchands adopted her when she was just days old."

Lord Newton covered his heart with his hand and leaned against the desk. "This is a blow. I didn't know this. Why is this not common knowledge? Is she trying to hide her antecedents? That is likely it; she is of low birth and does not want anyone to know. Are the . . ." He paled. "The Marchands . . . they are trying to ally themselves with our family. Of course; why did I not see it before?"

"What? How can you . . ."

"Our name, our title, our family history!" Lord Newton, his smooth cheeks pale but with a sheen of perspiration, trembled visibly. "Oh, that I have brought this shame down upon our family name! There is only one solution, of course."

Bert, stunned by the quicksilver shifts in his father's mood and reasoning, stood staring at the man. "What are you talking about, Father?"

"You must find a way out of this engagement . . . or . . . or I shall do it for you. That will serve. I will go now and tell the Marchands that it has been a mistake, and that you shouldn't suit after all, or . . ."

His stomach wrenched as if squeezed by an invisible fist. Bert cried, "You will do nothing of the kind! Father, I *want* to marry Miss Marchand!"

"But you can't!" The viscount frowned and twisted his mouth in a grimace. "They may sue for breach of promise, but if they do . . . we'll find a way to keep it quiet. We'll offer money. Or . . . I will merely point out to Mr. Marchand that our family's reputation will certainly stand up better than his, and that no monetary settlement can ever regain the girl's reputation once it is bandied about that she has done something that makes her unfit for . . ."

"*Father!*" Bert roared and glared at him, clenched fists at his side. If he ever felt like hitting his father, it was in that moment. "Hear me, and hear me good. You will say *nothing* to Sorrow, nor to her parents." His voice trembled, but he took a gulp of air and steadied himself. "And you will leave this house and not come back until the day before the wedding. Plead some emergency or something, but I will *not* have you speaking to my fiancée the way you just have been speaking *of* her."

"How dare you speak to me in that manner? I'll . . . I'll . . ."

"You'll what?"

Lord Newton's face was a portrait of indecision, his eyes narrowed. "I won't go. And unless you wish to enlighten the Marchands as to our subject this half hour, I don't think they'll see me ejected from their home when my son is marrying their daughter."

"You have to leave! I won't have Sorrow subjected to your venom."

"Bertram, it is not venom. And I wouldn't be rude to the girl; it's not her fault, after all. This is as much for her sake as it is for yours. I should have done more research before I pointed her out to you. But just listen, she will not be happy in London nor at Newton Castle, not once it is known . . ."

"Father, we won't be living either in London or at Newton Castle. Have you forgotten? Upon marriage, Hambelden Manor is mine. We'll live there."

There was silence in the library for a long few minutes. Bert could see that his father had indeed forgotten about his receipt, upon marriage, of his inheritance from his mother's parents. He could do nothing about it. It was one of the reasons Bert had been looking forward to marriage.

"You will defy me in this, I suppose."

"Yes. But don't think of it as defiance, for that means that I *should* listen to you but won't. In this case, Father, I think I'm in the right and you are wrong."

"But the Marchands . . . our family name . . ."

"They neither sought the alliance nor planned it. Remember, it was all our doing; you first pointed Sorrow out to me, and I courted her and asked her to marry me."

"Her odd name ought to have informed me there was something not quite right about the family."

"So will you be leaving?"

"No."

"Then you must behave in a proper manner to Sorrow, her parents, *and* the inhabitants of this household."

"I am who I am, Bertram," Lord Newton said, with the first glint of humor in his eyes that Bert had seen in a long time. "Have I ever, in your opinion, behaved in a proper manner? I think we define the word differently."

Against his conscience, Bert smiled, but then sobered immediately. "I'm serious, though, Father. I will not have you embarrassing me with any rudeness toward folks the Marchands consider their family."

"Fam . . . does that mean they will be coming to . . ." Lord Newton stopped talking. He shook his head. "I promise to behave in a proper manner, Bertram. But I will not leave. How would it look if I did?"

Hearing something in his father's voice that he didn't like, Bertram nonetheless knew his father enough to know that he would do as he said, to the letter. He examined the words for any subterfuge, any loophole that could be used to justify bad behavior, but gave up finally. He would have to handle what happened when it happened. Perhaps his father would be as good as his word, but he couldn't help feeling that Lord Newton was not completely done with any interference.

"Let's join the others, then," Bert said. "The family gathers before dinner for a cup of tea, and it is a chance for you to meet some of the others."

Sorrow, in the act of handing a cup of tea to Margaret, watched Bert and Lord Newton come into the parlor. From the expressions on their faces, she would guess it had not been a pacific meeting, and in fact Margaret had overheard shouting when she passed the library, she said.

In London Lord Newton had been very polite to her, if chilly in his behavior. Since that seemed to be his perpetual demeanor, though, she didn't take it personally.

Bert crossed to her immediately, nodded a polite

greeting to Margaret, and took Sorrow's hand. "May I speak to you privately?"

Margaret curtsied and moved away, considerately.

"I can't leave the tea table, Bert, but sit by me here and talk to me."

Her fiancé's gaze followed his father's perambulation of the room, she noticed. What was wrong between them? In London they had seemed to be at least polite to each other, but there was a tension here, like a wire pulled taut between them.

He took her hand in his and squeezed it. Just then Mr. William shuffled into the room and took a cup from the table, holding it out for Sorrow to fill it. She did so, and he ambled away to find a chair out of sight of the others in the room. Sorrow's mother and father were engaging Lord Newton in conversation, but the viscount stared at Mr. William with an odd look on his handsome face.

Sorrow turned back to her husband-to-be, though, and examined his eyes. "What's wrong, Bert? You seem overset."

"Sorrow," he said, turning to her. "If my father says or does anything to upset you, I want you to tell me."

Alarmed, she examined his expression, still searching his eyes to try to understand his worry. They were dark gray now, and his brows were drawn down, shadowing their depths. "What did you and your father talk about? Is . . . is anything wrong? Is your father all right?"

Bert laughed, a short, bitter bark of sound that drew attention. He turned away from the others and said, "He's fine, he's just his usual impossible self."

"What does that mean?"

Shaking his head, Bert didn't answer.

Sorrow watched Lord Newton. He appeared to be perfectly polite, but his gaze kept returning to Mr.

William, who shrank from the piercing gaze of the viscount.

That changed the moment Mrs. Liston entered.

Sorrow happened to be staring at Lord Newton and so saw him start, and his attention rivet. She glanced over and saw Mrs. Liston sweep in gracefully. She greeted Mr. William kindly, embraced Margaret, who gravitated to Mrs. Liston often, as to a second mother, and then made her way to the Marchands.

Sorrow turned and said to Bert, "Do you see your fa . . ." She didn't finish because he clearly *had* seen his father.

Lord Newton became a different man. He bowed before Mrs. Liston and his expression brightened from wintry to warmer, more like Bertram's. Sorrow could see the resemblance between father and son now.

In pantomime, from across the room, it appeared almost like a dance. He bowed, then he took the lady's hand and kissed the air about an inch above it as introductions were performed. He then set himself to be charming with an almost physical zeal.

"Apparently it takes an attractive woman to enter to make my father behave in a civil manner," Bert said, dryly.

"He appears much more than civil," Sorrow said, with a giggle.

Margaret approached them and Sorrow tugged at her sleeve. "What are they saying?"

"Lord Newton was talking about some people he knows in London, but then Mrs. Liston came in and he just stopped in mid word! It was the funniest thing!" She darted a glance at Bert and stuttered back into speech. "N-not that he was f-funny . . ."

"Don't worry, Miss Margaret," Bertram said,

kindly. "You may smile at his behavior all you like, for I have never seen the like, either. It is . . . interesting."

Sorrow nodded and chimed in. "Fascinating!"

CHAPTER SEVEN

Bertram had expected a miserable few days. He had expected disaster. He had expected every minute of every day that his father would say some horrible thing to disgust, disturb, or dismay the Marchands or their guests. But none of it had come to pass, and this moment, on a brilliant June day sitting in the garden on a stone bench, surreptitiously holding hands with Sorrow while his father walked with Mrs. Liston, Bert felt an absurd font of happiness well up in his heart.

"Billy's dragon is taking wing," he said, pointing with their jointly clasped hands at young Billy tending to his topiary.

Sorrow rubbed shoulders with him and smiled. She laid her cheek against his arm. "Bert, what would you do . . . I mean, if our child was born like Billy, what would you do?"

His stomach clutched. Was this some kind of test? He knew the story now, that Billy's mother, disgusted by her child's condition, had sent him away, though his father wanted to keep him home. There was money enough in the family to take care of him, it was just that his mother could not look at him without crying and she was afraid what their neighbors and relatives would think if they kept him at home.

The Marchands hoped, eventually, that the family would take him back.

Examining his own heart Bert wondered if, before meeting the Marchands and listening to his future father-in-law, he would immediately have answered that he would expect to send Billy to some family to care for him. It was what Society considered correct behavior, certainly. But did it serve? Billy's family was missing out on the company of a wonderful, intelligent, bright young lad because they could not bear the fact that he was born with no legs. Who lost most by such behavior?

"Bert?" Sorrow said, gazing up at him.

"I would hold him close and never let him go," Bert said, not recognizing his own voice, it was so clogged and quivering with emotion.

There was silence from Sorrow, but when he met her gaze it was to see her eyes shining with tears.

"Sorrow?"

"Oh, Bert, I . . . I love you!"

His heart was pierced with an arrow as sure as any legendary Cupid could have shot. He wished they were alone. He fervently wished they were already married, and he couldn't believe that a state he had only wished for to gain the independence of wealth he now looked forward to for much deeper reasons. He trembled. He wanted to take Sorrow into his arms, but they were in the garden, and it would shock many, mostly his father.

He pulled her into his arms anyway and kissed her on the mouth. Let his father be shocked. This perfect moment would never come again, and he would spend it as he wished.

* * *

Later in the day Sorrow, never forgetting her duties of the heart, sat by Miss Chandler's bed and stroked her frothy white hair back from her brow. But her mind wandered and she remembered with delicious clarity the moment of realization; she had said it, had told him. She loved Bertram Carlyle completely and devotedly.

That he had not responded in kind had caused a moment of fear, but she was determined not to let anything darken her happiness. Someday he would love her and someday he would tell her so.

The door pushed open and Mrs. Liston poked her head in. "May I come in, Sorrow?"

"Certainly! I was just talking to Miss Chandler."

The woman slipped in and sat down in the chair by Sorrow's. "I don't think she can hear you, dear."

"I know she doesn't perhaps understand, but I do think she hears my voice and that it soothes her."

When there was no response, Sorrow glanced over at the older woman. She was disturbed about something, that much was clear. But what brought her to Sorrow was *not* clear.

"What is it, ma'am?"

Mrs. Liston said, "Won't you call me Harriet? We have known each other quite long enough, I think."

Sorrow nodded and waited.

Harriet Liston looked down at her hands, folded on her lap, and bit her lip, frowning. It must be something to do with either her, Bert, or Lord Newton, Sorrow thought, for there to be such indecision on the woman's face.

"Is something wrong, ma'am? Harriet?"

She looked up, then, her blue eyes troubled. Sorrow knew that Harriet Liston was just a few years younger than her own mother, but though trouble had plagued her, she had the clear eyes and smooth skin of a younger woman. She had, since coming to the Marchands, sick, poor, and alone, recovered much of her youthful glow, but at that moment her complexion was pale instead of rosy, its normal hue.

"I . . . I don't want to cause trouble," she said.

Sorrow's stomach knotted. Nothing that started with those words could be good. Irrationally, she blamed the perfection of her earlier mood for the brewing storm, because nothing so perfect as her happiness could last. "Tell me what's wrong," she said, mustering what courage she could.

"I don't know Mr. Carlyle well enough to speak to him, and I suppose I shouldn't trouble you, so close to your wedding . . ." She stopped.

"Harriet," Sorrow said, taking her hand and holding it in both of hers, "tell me what's troubling you."

"It's Lord Newton. He . . . he seemed so gentlemanly at first, and he spoke to me with such consideration . . . but he has . . ." Her mouth worked and she trailed to a stop again.

"What has he done?"

"He won't believe me. He won't leave me alone. He has asked me to . . . oh, I'm so ashamed!" Harriet Liston looked down at her hand in Sorrow's and said, in a low tone, "He has asked me to be his mistress. I said no, but he thought I was being coy, and now he just says . . . he just says I *will* come to him."

Sorrow, fury building in her heart, said, "I'll take care of it. He won't bother you again, I promise it."

"Please, Sorrow, I don't want this to cause any trouble between you and your young man," Harriet said.

That concern caused her one moment of trepidation, but then a gladness filled her heart. She knew better now. She knew she could trust the man she loved. "No," she said. "It won't. Bert will know the right thing to do."

CHAPTER EIGHT

Bert and Sorrow, standing together in the garden, awaited Lord Newton, who had promised to join them.

Nuzzling her hair, Bert held Sorrow close, not even releasing her when Mr. William ambled past on his way to his preferred daily work of weeding the perennial hedge along the driveway. The old man smiled shyly at them and then bumbled away, meandering out the gate and down the drive to where he had left off the day before.

"Who is he?" Bert asked. "He dresses like a gardener, but takes part in the family meals."

"When he is here, he's just a man who likes to garden. When he is outside these walls he's a great politician . . . some have even said a future prime minister. If I told you his last name, you would recognize it."

"But . . ."

Sorrow whispered the name in his ear and he gazed down at her.

"Really?" Bert stared after the fellow. "But . . . he is known as an impassioned speaker—a crusader, some have said, for poverty reform. Even my father respects him, and that is saying much. Why would Father not recognize him here?"

"He looks different, Papa says, in his gardener clothing, and his demeanor is changed. He just finds the strain of his work too much sometimes. Once, a couple of years ago, he . . . I don't know, forgot who he was and wandered away. His valet followed him and then contacted Papa's valet, who was an acquaintance, to ask if Mama and Papa could help. They brought him here and he recovered. But they have found since that if he can just get away at the end of Parliament for a month or two—they put it about that he is at his estate working—then he can manage the terrible pressure of his work and perhaps do some good in Parliament."

Bert held Sorrow close and mused on the intricacies of life and the people. How many times had he seen someone in distress, or heard of a friend in trouble and done nothing? "I begin to think the world is an awful place, Sorrow, if so many people are in trouble or in pain. What do we do about them all? How can . . ."

Sorrow reached up and kissed his chin. "Bert, the truth is we can never help everyone. If you begin to think of how many people are in need, it will stop you from even trying because it seems so overwhelming. We can only help where we can. But the secret to it all is . . . well, it spreads from here. Years ago Papa helped a young man in need, and when he was able that man started an orphanage for climbing boys in London. Papa often says that man has helped more than he ever has, but that's how it works. You drop a pebble in the pond and the rings spread out and become bigger as they go."

"But does it always work? Aren't there some people who just can't be helped?"

"Of course. There has been sadness on occasion, and failures, but Papa says he just tries. Trying means that inevitably sometimes one fails. It's the way of life."

"I don't know if I'll ever be able to do what your father does, Sorrow. What if . . ."

She put one finger over his mouth. "Shush. Whatever comes has to come from the heart. You'll know when the time comes. I have faith in you, Bertram Carlyle, great faith."

Faith. She had faith in *him*? He didn't think anyone had ever said or thought that before, including himself. He just hoped he never disappointed her.

Lord Newton strode out of the door and spotted them together. His brows furrowed into two horizontal slashes, he stomped over to them.

Sorrow felt a momentary qualm. This was her father-in-law to be. What could she say to him about his behavior?

"Father," Bert said, his voice calm. He kept his arm around Sorrow's shoulders.

"What do you mean by asking me to come outside to talk like this?"

"It was the only way we could ensure we would not be overheard," Bert said. "Let's walk."

"No."

"All right."

Bert took a deep breath and Sorrow looked up at him. He could not be enjoying this moment, but from the second she told him of the viscount's behavior toward Mrs. Liston, he had insisted that he would be the one to talk to his father. He didn't want Sorrow there at all, but she said, quite rightly, that since Mrs. Liston had come to her, she should be there to hear what was said and affirm it.

The birds chirped gaily and the blue sky arched over them in cerulean perfection, but Sorrow clung to Bert, feeling a dark cloud had descended over her enjoyment of the day. Lord Newton had been the one element of her new marriage she was not looking forward to. He would be her second father, but a less fatherly man she had never met. Poor Bert.

"Well, out with it."

"Father, it has come to my attention . . ." He stopped.

"Spit it out!"

"You offended Mrs. Liston," he said, the words tumbling out of his mouth. "You . . . you, uh, said inappropriate things . . ."

Bert's palms were wet with sweat, Sorrow realized.

The viscount's face turned red and a vein bulged in his forehead. "I did no such thing! Who has told such monstrous lies?"

"Well, Mrs. Liston said that you offered . . . uh, offered her carte blanche . . ."

"Did she also tell you that I only did so after she kissed me in a most provocative way? I will thank you, Bertram and Miss Marchand—by the way Bertram, this is highly inappropriate, to be speaking of these things in front of your fiancée—to stay out of what does not concern you, or at least to get the story correct. If I had not had encouragement, I would never have made such a suggestion to Mrs. Liston. I would suggest to you that the widow is thinking to blackmail me into marriage."

"That is outrageous, Lord Newton, and I think you should apologize for even saying such a thing." Sorrow looked to Bert, but he was looking down at his feet and frowning. "Bert?"

"It could be a misunderstanding, Sorrow."

"No it couldn't!" Sorrow pulled away from Bert.

"But it could," Bert said, turning to her and trying to grasp her hands back in his. "I don't say that Mrs. Liston was trying to trap Father into marriage, but she

could have misunderstood, or he could have . . ."
Helplessly, Bert turned from his fiancée to his father
and back again. Both were staring at him. Neither was
willing to give an inch, or admit there might have been
a misunderstanding. Who to believe, though? He had
known Mrs. Liston for only a week or so, his father a
lifetime. If there was one thing his father was, it was
scrupulously truthful and with an exquisite sense of
fairness.

Usually.

"I did *not* misunderstand," the viscount said, his
whole body rigid with outrage, his voice choked with
rage. "How can one misunderstand a kiss such as I
have described?"

"Mrs. Liston didn't invite his insulting offer," Sorrow said, crossing her arms over her chest. "And
when she said no, he repeated the offer and would
not leave her alone."

Bert felt, in that moment, as though his future was
hanging in the balance. He stared at his father, and
in that second realized that much of what he had believed of his father over the years might be open to
interpretation. He had always seen his father's con-
frontations from that man's perspective, highly
colored by his own viewpoint. Lord Newton was reck-
oned to have a hasty temper, and Bert knew, from
personal experience, that his father was not good at
understanding an opposing point of view. He was
often, it had always seemed to Bert, led by his own
desires to believe that others thought or felt as he did
and was continually surprised and appalled when
they didn't.

Sorrow, on the other hand, had an exquisite sense
of justice, though she was not blind to human weak-
ness. Who should he believe? Who should he
support?

Even apart from the justice of the case, where did his allegiance now belong?

He took Sorrow's hand, a new gladness and confidence singing through his veins. He and his wife would be partners in life, there to weather whatever storms life should assault them with. "I think, Father, that you have an apology to make to the widow. You have offended her, whether you know it or not, and whether you intended to or not."

Lord Newton appeared puzzled. He glanced down at their joined hands and then at his son's face. He shook his head, turned, and walked away. But then he stopped, turned, and stared at them again. Silent for a long minute, his handsome face reflected bafflement, then decision. "Perhaps I have misunderstood," he said, stiffly. "I will apologize to Mrs. Liston."

CHAPTER NINE

There was still one more thing to be said, though. "We will bring Mrs. Liston here and you'll apologize," Bert said.

"I will apologize to her privately, though, Bertram, and not with you listening."

Bert gazed down at Sorrow and she nodded.

"We'll go and get her, sir," she said, squeezing Bert's hand.

They returned to the house.

"I would have insisted that he do so in front of us," Bert said, as they entered.

"I know," Sorrow said. "But there is something here I don't understand. Your father will keep his word, I know, won't he?"

"He is absolutely unwavering when he makes a promise. I was surprised he acquiesced, and so easily."

"I know. As I say, there's something here I don't understand. Let me find her and talk to her first," Sorrow said, leaving Bert in the hall and heading toward the stairs. She ran back, though, and gave him a kiss, shyly looking up and whispering, "I was proud of you out there," then heading back to the stairs.

Sorrow's mother was just coming from Mr. Howard's room. "Mama, where is Mrs. Liston?"

"In her room, dear." Mrs. Marchand caught her

daughter by the shoulders. "Sorrow, we've hardly had a chance to talk since Bert and his father have arrived. Is everything going all right?"

"Better. I wasn't sure at first, Mama, but . . . but Bert is the one! He's a good man."

"I know, dear. My only worry was that you expect so much! I was afraid you would reject him for being less than you expected and . . . oh, Sorrow, I do like him!"

They shared a quick hug. It was one thing she would miss sorely, this daily confabulation, the constant reassurance of her loving family. But that was all a part of moving on, of growing and becoming a woman. She had to be grateful a man like Bert was to be her companion.

As her mother disappeared down a turn in the hall, Sorrow moved in the opposite direction and found Harriet Liston's room. She tapped, then obeyed the summons to enter.

The lady was folding some clothes and placing them carefully in a trunk.

"What are you doing?" Sorrow asked.

The lady looked up and smiled. "Since your father has so very kindly procured my pension for me, I'll be moving out. I am going to move back north to Durham, closer to where I grew up."

"But you don't have anyone there."

"No, but my life is moving on now, just as yours is. I came here ill and broken and poor, and your father and mother have done so very much. I will never be able to repay them. Nor you!"

Sorrow crossed the room and gave the woman a quick hug. "Yes, you will. You know all Father ever asks anyone who leaves is just to pass on the kindness somehow. No grand gestures, just kindness. It's enough."

Harriet Liston hugged her close, seeming not to want to let go. When she did release her, it was to stare at her and say, "I wish I had had a daughter like you. I wish my children had survived."

Sorrow knew her story, the miscarriages and the lone surviving child who had died within months of her husband. It was those events, so close to each other, that had finally cast her into such a pit of depression that she had been close to death herself, just from wasting away. She had been at Spirit Garden for almost two years now, and her health was now glowing, her spirit raised to hope and determination.

Sitting down on her bed, Sorrow knew there was no response for the woman's longing. She was not destined to have children, it seemed, and most of the time had learned to accept that.

"Harriet, we spoke to Lord Newton."

She returned to her folding and said, "And what did he have to say?"

"He said you kissed him, and that is where he got the idea you would acquiesce."

She was silent.

"Did you kiss him?" Sorrow asked, trying to catch a glimpse of the woman's expression.

Straightening, Harriet defiantly said, "Yes, I did. We . . . he . . . we walked often in the garden, and it was the first time since my husband died that . . . that a man had paid attention to me. It was nice. He was kind. I thought . . . I thought . . ." She looked down at the scarf in her hands and shook her head. "I was mistaken. What a fool I've been! He is Lord Newton, a viscount, and I'm just a poor soldier's widow. I should have known how he would interpret my complaisance."

"But you kissed him," Sorrow insisted, trying to understand. "*He* says provocatively."

The woman sighed and laid the scarf in the trunk and closed the lid, carefully, quietly. She sat down on it. "No." She met Sorrow's gaze. "No, not provocatively. I kissed him as a woman does who finds a man attractive and thinks he cares for her, too. I was wrong."

Hearing the bitterness in the woman's voice, Sorrow reached out and rubbed her shoulder. "I'm sorry. He will apologize, though. He's waiting outside."

The two women joined Bert in the hall and exited the house. Lord Newton was staring down at the stream below, and at the willow that tossed in the light June breeze. He turned, hearing them crunch on the gravel, and his expression was one of confusion.

As they approached, he said, "Mrs. Liston, I have an apology to make, but to do it properly, I would talk to you alone for a moment."

She glanced uncertainly back at Sorrow and Bert.

"Father, you can apologize in front of us," Bert said.

"No," Harriet Liston said, buoyed by their support. "His lordship can say whatever he wants, privately or publicly." Her chin went up in defiance and she nodded when he took her arm. They strolled away, but not too far.

Sorrow and Bert watched the pantomime. Lord Newton spoke for a long minute, and then Harriet Liston nodded and turned to walk away, but he grasped her elbow and made some sort of plea.

She shook her head, but he insisted. She finally acquiesced and listened to him some more.

"What do you think they're talking about?" Sorrow asked.

"I don't know," Bert said. "But . . . I've never seen my father so . . . I don't know . . . involved. Impassioned."

"What do you mean?"

"It appears that he really cares what she thinks. I

think . . . I think he's arguing his case, apologizing, but saying something more."

As they watched, Mrs. Liston shook her head, moved away from him, and then looked back, to say one more thing. Then she turned and headed back to the house, but by another route, as if she didn't want to talk to anyone just then. Lord Newton, his expression grim, stomped toward them.

"This household," he said, when he reached them, "is mad. Absolutely incorrigibly mad!" He stared at Bert. "If you marry this young woman, you will live exactly the same way, with dying people and invalids and lunatics. I do not understand how you can even consider it, but I *will not* stay and countenance you joining our old and dignified family name with this . . . with this lunacy!" With that he stomped away.

The apology, it seemed, had not gone well.

"Does he mean he'll leave before the wedding?" Sorrow said, gazing up at her fiancé.

"Maybe," Bert said, grimly watching his father's retreat. "But he will apologize yet again—this time to you—before he goes, or I won't be speaking to him any time in the foreseeable future."

Bert stomped off after his father, leaving Sorrow staring after them. What had happened? How had her lovely wedding turned into this divisive, acrimonious, angry event?

CHAPTER TEN

Sorrow paced in the garden. Things seemed to have gone from bad to worse, with her wedding set for the next day. Lord Newton, when Bert had demanded an apology, said he would rather leave than either apologize or be an inmate of such an impossible place for another minute. He was expected to leave that afternoon.

Harriet Liston was staying for the wedding, she said, but would not be in the same room with Lord Newton, who had, apparently, apologized, but then tried to explain why he felt he was offering her a valuable boon by offering her the position of mistress to him. He had made it sound, Harriet said, as if he was offering a chambermaid a spot in his household.

Bert was moody and unhappy, and Sorrow didn't know how to make it any better. Surely this was not the way to start a marriage.

Her mother and father came up the garden walk toward her, arm in arm and with identical serious expressions on their faces.

"Sorrow, is everything all right between you and young Bertram?" her father asked.

The two flanked her and pulled her to them in a

hug. She buried her face in her father's neck. "Yes. No. Not exactly."

"Why don't we sit down?" Sorrow's mother said. "We haven't had a chance for a family talk for a while."

They sat together on a bench in the garden, with gray clouds scudding overhead across the stormy sky. Rain threatened, and Sorrow felt as though the dismal weather was reflecting her own mood. She had thought everything would be so simple once she decided that Bertram Carlyle was the right man for her and he proposed. What else was there to worry over? But now it seemed that the mere act of becoming engaged had driven a wedge between Bert and his father. When she had tried to express her concern over that, Bertram had merely said that the wedge was always there, but he had never noticed it before. She wasn't to worry, he said. It was Lord Newton's problem, not hers.

But she did worry. Harmony was a guiding principle in her own life, and how could one live harmoniously with such bad feeling, and especially when it was her very own wedding which was causing so much trouble?

"Sorrow," her mother said, "you don't have to marry on Friday. You don't have to marry at all, if it is a worry to you."

"But I *want* to marry Bert," Sorrow said. "And I want his father to approve. Bert says it doesn't matter, but I think it does."

"However, my dear, the problem is really between Lord Newton and his son," her father said. "I don't think it has anything to do with you, or even with us and how we live. I think Lord Newton has been shocked at how young Bertram has matured, and it bothers him. Perhaps he didn't realize until now that his son is a grown man and will no longer be under his thumb."

"I just don't want my wedding to be marred by unpleasantness. It's supposed to be the happiest day of my life."

"Then you have a decision to make, my dear," her mother said, laying a kiss on her brow. "You must decide whether you will go ahead or if this is all too hurtful, and then you must tell Bertram he either solves his differences with his father or the wedding is canceled. We love you and want you to be happy, but it is your wedding, after all."

"I know. I want to think about it, and then I want to talk to Bert about it."

"That's wise," her father said, standing and pulling his wife to her feet. "Whatever you decide, we will support."

"I'm a fortunate girl. The things I heard from other girls in London . . . I came back to Spirit Garden knowing what a lucky girl I am. Most parents would not behave as you, you know?"

"Maybe not, but they should, if they loved their daughter," her father said. He took his wife's arm and they strolled away. "Just tell us in time to let the vicar know," he said, over his shoulder.

It was later in the day and Sorrow still didn't know what to do. The day had turned sunny, the sun burning off the gloom to reveal another brilliant June day. She was not alone, for one of the footmen had carried old Mr. Howard out to enjoy the sunshine, that being one of the pleasurable sensations that he craved.

She held his hand and he squeezed it every once in a while, his weathered face turned up to the sun, his almost sightless eyes closed. When he had first come to them he was still able to speak, but now he was wordless, but not, she knew, without feeling. And hearing. She talked to him often.

"What am I going to do, Mr. Howard? Bertram . . . you've seen how wonderful he is. He's everything I hoped for and feared never to find. I don't think he even realizes that yet. But his father . . . he's going to make Bert miserable."

The old man squeezed her hand.

"I know. I'm marrying Bert, not his father. But I want them to be . . . friends. And I want Lord Newton to approve of me for his son. I'm afraid he doesn't now."

She looked up from Mr. Howard's face just then and saw the viscount striding toward her. Her companion squeezed her hand more firmly and she clung to it, drawing strength from the old man's love.

Lord Newton stopped before her, cast one irritated glance at the old man in his Bath chair, and then glared at Sorrow.

"Walk with me, Miss Marchand."

"Whatever you wish to say to me can be said in front of Mr. Howard." The old man squeezed her hand.

The viscount cast a disgusted look at her companion. "All right. This won't take long. When I first saw you, I thought you would do for Bertram. You are not too young, nor is your family of the first stare. Bertram needed a lady with a little more . . . sense than some of the young girls in London. I thought you were that one."

Sorrow did not feel the need to say anything. The viscount's implication was clear; he had been wrong about some things, among them Sorrow's good sense.

The viscount paced on the flagstone pathway, not even seeming to see the lovely garden, or feel the sweet warmth of the sun. "But I was not apprised of many things concerning your background and your family. I have been sorely misled. I did not know you are only an adopted daughter to the Marchands and not their real daughter."

Ire bit into Sorrow, but she pushed it back. She drew her hand away from Mr. Howard, not wanting to communicate her anger to her old friend. Lord Newton's opinion did not mean a thing to her, she tried to tell herself.

"Nor did I know of this . . . this utter chaos that the Marchands choose to live in!" He waved his hands around, encompassing the house and the garden and by implication all the members.

He stopped and glared down at her. "How can you live like this? And how can you . . . how can you . . ." He waved a hand at Mr. Howard. "I will not countenance this marriage, nor will I attend the wedding. I am leaving. I will never understand how you can live in this disorder and deal with . . . with such people."

"Perhaps you're right, my lord, about one thing. You will never understand if you can look at Mr. Howard, here, and say such things. Look at his face," she said, leaning forward. "Look at him."

The viscount reluctantly did so.

She put out one hand and traced the wrinkles on the old man's face. His filmy eyes opened and he smiled at Sorrow, putting one gnarled and ancient hand over her young one. Quietly, Sorrow said, "There is so much terrifying beauty and dignity in his pain. I don't know how else I can explain it. Ugliness and death . . . they are a part of life and when embraced . . . they're beautiful, too. I don't mean in and of themselves; that would be sophistry, for there is nothing beautiful in our end *except* what we have learned and given back to this world. But just look at the acceptance in his eyes, the patience. It's glorious and humbling." She patted his cheek and straightened, turning back to the viscount. "When I met Bertram I knew he would understand that. I don't know how I knew, I just did. He had . . ."

She paused, searching for the right words as the viscount stared at her in incomprehension. How to express to this man, who had so long denigrated his son, that there was one person in the world who thought Bertram everything fine and noble? "My lord, your son has a more powerful spirit than any man I ever met in London or anywhere else. When I look deep into his eyes I see . . . I see my future. If you don't know that about him, if you don't understand what a fine man he is, then I pity you, sir. I sincerely pity you."

A movement caught her eye and she saw that Bertram had been nearby and likely heard her. He stared at her, and there was such a speaking look of love in his eyes that it took her breath away. Lord Newton looked from one of them to the other, and as Bertram made his way toward Sorrow, his eyes never leaving hers, Lord Newton shook his head.

"I don't understand." His voice held genuine bewilderment.

"Maybe you never will," Bert said, as he joined Sorrow and took her hand.

Lord Newton stared at them both. "You will go ahead with this marriage, even against my wishes?" he said to his son.

Bert just smiled. "I think you know better than to even ask. Why would I leave Sorrow? I'm a fortunate man that you happened to point out to me the one woman in the world who makes me . . ." He turned his gaze to Sorrow, and finished, "whole. And happy."

"You are both doomed to unhappiness, don't you see that?"

Sorrow looked back up at the viscount and met his troubled gaze. She was stricken by the expression of utter perplexity on his handsome visage. "No, we aren't. How can you not understand?"

"Sir, it's more than just love," Bertram said, sure now of his feelings. "Though I know for most people the . . . the love we . . . we share would be enough . . ." He looked down at his bride-to-be and his voice choked off for a moment as he gazed into her beautiful eyes. He couldn't believe what he was feeling and thinking, it had hit him so forcefully. She truly loved him, and he had fallen in love with her. But there was more . . . so much more! She *chose* him. She didn't just blindly acquiesce to an eligible offer of marriage. And she chose him because she thought him to be more than even he thought himself to be, a man with a good and true heart, a man who could do anything.

She believed in him, and he knew now that he couldn't live without that.

Her face, upon hearing his words, his admission of love, glowed with astonished joy. He realized he had never even told her he loved her yet. How much they had to talk about! How much he had to tell her of all the new discoveries in his heart.

But first, his father.

"I can't put into words what it feels like, Father, to know that Sorrow isn't marrying me because I will one day be Viscount Newton. Nor is she marrying me because I'm wealthy. Nor because she is afraid no one else will ask her. Somehow she knew—and I'm so grateful to her, for I have been blind for too long—that in each other we have found our soul's true mate."

Lord Newton was silent. He shook his head and stared at Sorrow, then at his son. "I won't pretend to understand. I don't."

"Father," Bertram said, pouring all of his hope into his tone. "If you would open your heart to Spirit Garden and to the people here, to Mr. Howard and Billy and poor Joshua . . ."

"Good God, do not counsel me to hobnob with madmen and invalids," the viscount said. He turned away, but then turned back again and gazed at the young couple. Bert had taken Sorrow's hand in his and she had caught up Mr. Howard's hand again. "I . . . I just don't understand."

He walked away.

"Bert," Sorrow said, leaning against him, "will he ever understand?"

"I don't know," he said, "and his attitude may sadden us, but we can't live for him." His heart thudded and he couldn't contain the bubbling spring of purest joy that welled up in him despite the chasm between his father and himself. "Mr. Howard," he said, "will you excuse us for a few moments? I would like to . . . would like to tell my bride of all the discoveries I've made and it's . . . it's a private moment."

He could see the old man's hand flex around Sorrow's, and she said, "He says all right, but to behave ourselves!"

She giggled and Mr. Howard smiled and nodded.

Bert led her away, out of the garden and to the long green grassy slope and pulled her to him, finding her lips, kissing her softly, then with increasing passion. How would he ever explain the feelings coursing through him? No man had ever felt like this in all the years of creation.

"Sorrow," he murmured into her hair, "I love you. My soul has been reborn and I love you. I'm such a lucky man to have found you and then to have convinced you to marry me. I didn't love you then. What blind stupid luck that you said yes!"

"No, not luck. Bert, I didn't say yes with no notion of our future. I *knew* this day could happen. I just didn't know you would be so intelligent as to discover you could love me so quickly!"

They chuckled together and gazed deeply into each other's eyes. The light breeze riffled through her curls and he pushed back her stray tendrils. "You really saw something in me, something no one else had ever seen, not even me or my father."

"Especially not your father," she said, with a trace of acerbity in her voice.

"Let's not talk about him," Bert said.

"I will agree to that. Bert, you will marry me anyway, won't you, even though your father doesn't approve?"

"You could not push me away if you tried. I have had a taste of heaven, and I want to pass through the gates."

Another few moments were lost in kissing.

"Then let's get married."

"I think we will," Bert said, and, putting his arm around her, walked back toward the house. They had more plans to make.

CHAPTER ELEVEN

The viscount didn't leave, and for the rest of the day he was seen pacing in the garden, talking to various folks who lived or worked in the house, and sometimes to the Marchands themselves. Often, just on his own, he walked in the meadow.

Sorrow saw him from her window, and it tinged her day with sadness to know that there was that rift between Bert and his father.

She didn't sleep well.

Margaret came in to her early—the wedding breakfast after the ceremony was a morning affair in the garden, of course—and sat on her bed. "How are you this morning, Sorrow?" she asked, shyly.

She was already dressed in her new lavender gown, filled with nervous anticipation of her role as bride's attendant, and her hands were elegantly gloved.

"I'm tired," Sorrow said truthfully, yawning hugely. "I don't think I slept at all."

"Nervous, I should think," Margaret returned blushing. "I would be, to think that this evening . . . you will be . . . I mean . . ."

"Hmm? Oh, well, yes, I am a little nervous about that, but Mama has told me there is nothing to be afraid of, you know."

"Really?"

She looked so disbelieving that Sorrow almost laughed, but was saved by a desire not to hurt Margaret's feelings, which were often raw and close to the surface. "Really. Mama says it is a little uncomfortable at first when you . . . when . . . well, you know what I mean. But she says it is quite pleasant after a while. She said it's nothing to be afraid of."

Margaret looked relieved, but still doubtful. "My mother said it is a torment and that men are brutes once they shed their clothes. She said it is the price women pay for the Original Sin, you know, that and childbirth."

"And when was your mother ever truthful with you or right about anything?"

Her expression brightened. "That's true! My mother has been wrong about other things, too. And your mother always tells the truth. Anyway, we shouldn't be talking about such things. So if that is not worrying you, what is?"

"It's this quarrel between Bert and his father. I feel . . . responsible."

"But your father told your mother that it is Lord Newton's disagreeable personality that is at fault, and that he could never imagine how such a sterling young man came from such a father."

"My father said that to my mother in front of you?"

"They . . . they didn't know I was there. But I wasn't eavesdropping, truly, Sorrow, I was in a club chair in the library and didn't want to interfere when I heard them come in."

"Margaret!"

The girl began to twist her hands together, but then stopped and said, "I know . . . I should have stood and let them know I was there. I'll . . . I'll try not to be so shy next time."

"Especially with Mother and Father!" Sorrow turned

back to her own problems and wished things were different. Lord Newton, in London, had seemed distant but polite. She had just thought him frosty, but now it seemed to her that he had layered his distressing lack of compassion and empathy under a veneer of civilized behavior. How had he turned out a son like Bert? It was a miracle and a blessing, but she would still be his daughter-in-law for the rest of his life and they would have to deal with each other on a continuing basis. And if she had children—

She buried her face in the covers over her knees and felt Margaret's hand on her head.

"You're probably just nervous," she said, lightly. "I'll call the maid. Your mama said you have to get up and get dressed."

The door closed as Margaret left.

It was more than just bride nerves, Sorrow thought, lifting her head and facing her fears. Harmony, that guiding principle in her life, was threatened. She didn't know if she could go ahead without it.

Another hour and he would be a married man, Bert thought, pacing anxiously in a quiet part of the enclosed lawn. The ceremony was to be in the tiny ancient chapel beyond the garden, and then the couple would come out to the company and be announced as husband and wife. Then there would be a grand breakfast with the inmates of the house and villagers and invited guests, too, as well as some relatives all mixing in a grand mélange. The seating was already arranged, tables flowing with white cloths fluttering in the breeze.

Bert had thought he would despise this kind of public celebration, but on joining his life with Sorrow's, he felt he was gaining an extended family of such warmth as he had never in his life experienced. He looked up from his contemplation to see his father advancing toward him. He was dressed for the ceremony, so he must have decided to stay. Bert was not sure how he felt about that.

"Bertram," Lord Newton said, "I need to talk to you."

"Yes?"

The viscount glared off in the distance, furrowed his brow, and said. "I don't quite know how to say this, but . . ."

"Then don't. Father, I thought that I needed your approval . . ."

"Bertram . . ."

"No! Let me say this," Bert said, putting up one hand. "All my life I did most of what you told me. I did well in school. I shot, I fenced, I hunted. I courted the girls of whom you approved. And then, by the greatest chance in the world, I met Sorrow. I think now what a fool I was not to make an effort to get to know her before you pointed her out to me, but I feel certain now that even if you hadn't, we would have come together. Apparently she saw me and liked me before I ever noticed her. We were meant to be together.

"And now you cannot turn me away from her. I love her and we are going to marry today with or without your blessing."

Lord Newton stared at him, and a smile twisted his lips. At least Bert thought it might be a smile, being unfamiliar with that expression on his father's face.

"You really should let me speak, you know, for I . . ."

"Mr. Carlyle!"

Bert turned to see Billy being wheeled toward him by Joshua. "What is it, Billy?"

"Sorrow wants to see you upstairs. She sent me 'specially . . . said it was important."

"All right, thank you, young fellow. I'll be back down in a few minutes, Father, and we can continue this conversation if you wish."

"I do wish," Lord Newton said. "You and I have much to discuss. But in the meantime Billy, Joshua, and I will stroll in the garden."

Bert stopped and turned back, the words startled him so much, but his father was already walking along the stone path and questioning Billy about his dragon bush. It was a sight he never would have imagined possible and gave him much food for thought, though he didn't have time for it at that minute.

His bride-to-be needed him.

He raced up the stairs and saw Mrs. Liston on the landing. "Is Sorrow . . ."

"In her room, Mr. Carlyle. Go in. She said she needs to talk to you."

He entered the door he had long known was to her room—long known and tried to forget—and saw her, as she turned from the window, the sun touching her golden curls and glinting off the iridescent pale yellow of her gown.

"You're beautiful," he said, coming across the room to her.

She held him at arm's length. "Bert, I thought it didn't matter."

"What?"

"I thought your father's approval or disapproval didn't matter, but it does. I can't do it, not without him approving of it."

"What?" He knew he was repeating himself stupidly, but he felt all the blood drain from his heart, it felt like, and that organ thudded uncomfortably. It was just like a nightmare, that what he wanted—needed—more than water and sunshine was snatched away just as he reached out his hand. "You can't mean that."

"But I do," she said, tears welling in her eyes. "I've thought about it all night and all morning, but I can't! I know how much he means to you! If my father didn't approve . . ."

"You wouldn't marry me?"

"I don't know, I don't *know!*"

They stared at each other.

"He will approve," Bert said, through clenched teeth. "If that is what you need to become my bride this morning, then he *will* approve."

"But you can't force approval . . ."

"Never mind, Sorrow. He will."

He gave her a quick kiss, then a more lingering one, and raced back down to the garden. His father was standing alone watching Mrs. Liston, who was guiding a couple of ladies from the village to a table in the shade.

"She won't marry me!"

"I beg your pardon?" Lord Newton said, turning.

"Sorrow," he grated out between clenched teeth. "She won't be the cause of a rift between us, she says, because she knows that you are important to me. She will have your approval or she won't marry me. You *will* approve, sir, and you will tell her so!"

"Is that any manner to speak to your father?" Lord Newton's eyes were wintry.

"I don't care. I won't beg, I won't plead, but you *will* do this." He glared at his father, and the wintry look in Lord Newton's gray eyes melted.

His voice oddly gentle, he said, "I will."

He moved to pass by Bert, but Bert caught his sleeve.

"What?"

"I'm going to tell my future daughter that she must marry you."

It was the oddest day, Bert thought. Everything predictable was upside down. He gave his head a shake. "Why?"

"How dull you are being, Bertram. Of all the things I ever thought of you, I never thought you a dullard."

"I mean, you don't approve. Why are you doing this? Just because I want you to?"

"No. How do you know I don't approve?"

"Because you told me so yesterday."

"Ah, but have you never heard of a sea change? I never thought such a thing could happen to me, but it has. I . . ." He paused, and the oddest expression of discovery crossed his handsome face. "I took your advice—something I have never done before, you will note—and I spent yesterday talking to people, to young Billy and Mr. Marchand and an old *old* lady named Mrs. Mackintosh. She told me I was a great ass, and that anyone could see the young people were so in love it would be the making of my son; a good woman, she said, while she cannot change a man, can bring out in him the best that is there. And Sorrow was the very best of young women, and young Bertram, she insisted, the very best of young men."

Bert stared at his father. "I can't quite believe it is you saying these things. People just do not change overnight."

"No, I suppose you're right." He sounded tired and looked discouraged, but then brightened. "Tomorrow I will likely be my old incorrigibly overbearing self, so take advantage of this softer . . ." The viscount stopped speaking, looked away and watched Mrs. Liston. "If I had heard Mrs. Mackintosh's advice thirty years ago, I might have married differently, who knows? There was a woman who loved me, but she told me no, that I was too pompous for her taste. Like a fool, I let her slip away." He mused for a moment. "What would I have become if I had found the courage to go after her? She was unsuitable in so many ways, I remember . . . gloriously unsuitable! But I cannot lament, can I? Your mother was a good woman and bore you, and that was an excellent thing for the world."

"Then you'll go to Sorrow?"

"I will. She would be a great fool not to marry you. You're a good man."

Bert, stunned, stood stock still as Lord Newton passed him, clapping him on the shoulder in as great a show of affection as he had ever given, and then entered the house.

Sorrow paced up and down her room. Her gloves were in a damp heap on her dressing table and she was alone, having told her mother and Margaret that she needed a moment.

There was a tap at the door and she turned, saying, "Come in."

Lord Newton entered.

Involuntarily, she found herself thrusting her chin up and donning an expression of defiance. He wouldn't like what she had to say.

He cleared his throat and just barely entered the room. "Bertram told me . . . that is . . ."

"That I wouldn't marry him without your approval."

"That's right."

"I've changed my mind. I've been sitting here

thinking, and I will *not* let you ruin my day and our lives."

"But, my dear . . ."

"Don't call me that, my lord, when it is quite clear to me that you neither like nor approve of me and my family. But I won't give him up, and if you reject him . . . reject *us* . . . then I will work that much harder to make him as happy as he deserves. I love him too much. I won't let him go."

The viscount smiled. "I am relieved to hear it, my dear. But really, there is no need for such vehemence. You will become wrinkled if you frown so fiercely."

"I . . . I beg your pardon?"

"My whole life, Miss Marchand . . . Sorrow . . . I have felt that the dignity of our family name was so great that I, and then Bertram when his time comes, must serve it, like serfs, you know. It required certain things of us, and one was to comport ourselves with great dignity. Another was to marry properly, a girl who would go along with our beliefs. I was misled by your mild London behavior to think you such a girl."

"And now?"

"Now, I have undergone a change, and begin to think I should turn things around and make my name and position serve me, not the other way around."

Sorrow felt a great weight slip from her shoulders. "Does this mean you . . . you approve?"

"I do, and so I have told Bertram, though he was willing to badger me into approving just to convince you to marry him. He is greatly in love with you, and I can't say that I blame him. You are an adorable girl and . . . and a valuable addition to our family."

She flew at him on an impulse and wrapped her arms around him, hugging him so hard they both rocked backward. He laughed, at first stiffly, sounding like a creaky gate, and then in great whoops.

"How lucky I am you are not a young lady to hold grudges."

"So I can see I am either to be a groom this day, or acquire a new stepmother. Which is it to be?"

Sorrow peeked around the viscount and saw Bert standing just inside the door, lounging against the doorjamb. She never would have expected such dry wit from him, and realized she still had much to learn about Bertram Carlyle. And many years, if they were lucky, in which to do it. She felt a shiver of anticipation race down her spine.

"Father, will you leave us alone for a minute?" he said, with an odd anticipatory gleam in his gray eyes.

"No," the viscount said, taking Sorrow's arm and guiding her from the room. "You two will have time enough for all you want to say. But first, I will see you married."

Most of the folks gathered for the breakfast tried to crowd into the tiny chapel, and there was much rustling and talking and laughter. The old house of worship had not seen service as a wedding chapel in many years, and most of the villagers had never seen the interior, so there was that to be discussed, too. Joshua danced in the aisles while Billy laughed, and the brilliant sunlight streamed through the ancient stained glass windows, throwing colorful patterns over the congregation.

Lord Newton would allow no one but himself to carry in Mr. Howard, who smiled through the entire ceremony, while Mrs. Marchand cried and Mr. Marchand tried not to. The solemnity of the vows was interrupted many times, and in many ways.

Harriet Liston, Sorrow noticed, could not help but gasp when she saw Lord Newton's new behavior.

Tears sparkled in her eyes in the dim chapel light when he held Billy on his lap temporarily, so the boy could see the ceremony. It was too much of a change, Sorrow almost felt, but it continued through the day, while toasts were made repeatedly, through the long riotous wedding breakfast that stretched late into the afternoon.

But finally the day was done. Exhausted, Sorrow changed into a traveling dress, visited the old people, each in turn, and kissed Miss Chandler what she knew would be a last good-bye. A posy from Sorrow's wedding bouquet adorned the old lady's bedside table. She descended and Billy and Joshua, Letty, Nancy Smith, Mr. William . . . all had their moment.

She spent a half hour alone with her father and mother, where the tears flowed freely, tears which mingled with laughter and reminiscing. The Marchands would miss her, but knew with Bertram she would be all right.

And finally, as the sky turned pink-gold and the brick of Spirit Garden a deep umber, she joined her husband in the carriage that was to carry them the short distance to Dover and their hotel for the first night of their marriage. The next day they would board a boat for Europe and their wedding trip.

"Look," Sorrow said, as they pulled away from Spirit Garden, down the lane. "Your father has Mrs. Liston on his arm. Do you think . . ."

"What? Do I think that my father and the widow would make a fine couple, if she'll have him? And that perhaps she will be just as good for him as you are for me?"

Sorrow, laughing, turned around in her seat and snuggled close to her new husband. "I think I'll stop now, for you are far too adept at reading my mind. Or no . . . one more time. What am I thinking now?"

Bertram slipped his arms around her waist and pulled her closer to him. "That we cannot get to the hotel in Dover nearly quickly enough." He nuzzled her ear.

She chuckled, a throaty murmur of sound. "Almost right, Mr. Carlyle. I was thanking your brilliant foresight in getting a closed carriage for the short trip, and wondering if the shades pull all the way down."

"Do you even have to ask?" Bert said, putting the answer to her question into action. The shades drawn, the carriage was pleasantly dim, and there were a few moments with no sound but the occasional giggle and some rather raspy breathing.

"I hope Dover is not far," Sorrow finally said.

"I hope," Bert fervently agreed.